***The Colony***
**a Vardan Herkth story**

A sorcerer in a peaceful land is confronted with a sorcerer from a warlike land. There are strange plant-people from another place who are trapped by the machinations of the evil sorcerer.

Can Var and his barbarian sidekick, Dracht, face and defeat this monster, even with the help of the apprentice sorcerer, Von?

# Contents

# About the author

CD Moulton has traveled extensively over much of the world both in the music business, where he was a rock guitarist, songwriter and arranger and in an import/export business. He has been everything from a bar owner to auto salvage (junkyard) manager, longshoreman to high steel worker, orchid grower to landscaper, tropical fish farmer to commercial fisherman. He started writing books in 1983 and has published more than 250 books as of January 1, 2015. His most popular books to date are about research with orchids, though much of his science fiction and fantasy work has proven popular. He wrote the CD Grimes, PI series and the Det. Nick Storie series, Clint Faraday series and many other works.

He now resides in Gualaca,Chiriqui, Panamá, where he writes  books, plays music with friends, does research with orchids and medicinal plants – and pursues his favorite pastime roaming the mountain jungles doing his botanical research. He has lately become involved in fighting for the rights of the indigenous people, who are among his closest friends, and in fighting the extreme corruption in the courts and police in Panamá.

He offers the free e-book, *Fading Paradise*, that explains what he has been through because of the corruption.

CD is the discoverer of the Chadam Protocol for curing cancer. Facebook page: Ambrosia peruviana for cancer.

## *The Colony*

### *Prologue*

Vardan Herkth looked out the observation dome on the new station and sighed deeply.

Something was not right here. Something from another place, an undefined place of some sort, was influencing the people.

He had powers. It was his function here to use those powers to protect the people of the land, his sworn duty to his king (who he felt was probably a good enough person, for a king, but was not exactly the greatest intellect in the castle – by a very wide margin) and his people. In a choice between serving King Narjur and the people, Narj, as he was called, would find himself a very distant second spot winner.

That was one good thing about the power. No one dared challenge him, not that Narj would. He was well-aware of his weaknesses and did honestly care about the people.

Var was getting old, on the "normal" scale of things, but his powers weren't diminished. Another hundred years and he'd have to train the next Sorcerer of the Realm. Two hundred fifty years were enough to ask of anyone. He was quite sure he would welcome his time of passing, when it came.

There was the tingle. A portal – a very large one – was being held opened somewhere ... that way. Var turned to face toward the Sawteeth Mountains rising on the late afternoon horizon across the wide silver lake. What was this? What was happening there that made the feeling of ... not evil. Difference. Alienity was more the word for it.

Well, if a portal to Nighkt were being opened, some very truly alien things could come through. Var wasn't sure, by any measure, that anyone here could hope to understand the beings there.

As an apprentice, himself, he had traveled to Nighkt with Vardan Melkth, his predecessor. He had seen nothing, other than very strange dry landscapes and plants, but had felt the entire time he was there that he was watched from somewhere just beyond the limits of his vision – or perhaps from something he was not capable of seeing, only of sensing.

There was much the same feeling here. It is what made him think of Nighkt.

Whatever it may be, it did not belong on Kholworld, much less in a place like Fendrz.

Chapter one

"Ah! My Lord Vardan!" King Narjur greeted, as Var (He had been called the nickname for "Vardan" since he was appointed Sorcerer to the Realm by Queen Garjur, grandmother of King Narjur, more than one hundred years ago and had served under King Qarjur, father of King Narjur) came into the court.

Var had been friends with them all and had understood them. It was a good family to rule. Unlike so many – far too many – in the long history of Kholworld, even in Fendrz, this family actually cared about the people. Fendrz could have a king like King Hopjur in Gretlz, who used all the resources of Gretlz in building a large army.

Hopjur could use the intelligence to train and appoint a more decent sorcerer and his adventures might find some measure of success. That was certain *not* to happen so long as he feared loss of power. If he lost power his family would perish. The people of Gretlz would rise to avenge themselves of generations of suppression.

Someday Hop – or a descendant – would again turn to an adventure against Fendrz and Var would be forced to quash them, which would lead to Fendrz being forced to take charge of the affairs of that huge land. King Narjur would be among the first to agree that he had little ability to do so, as the military psychology was alien to him – as alien as that ... whatever ... in the mountains was to Var.

"Your Highness," Var returned, nodding his respect. This was a form that must be followed in the court, but would be ignored outside of formal functions of the realm, where they would meet as friends. "There is a problem that demands my attentions?"

"I'm not certain, Lord Vardan," Narj replied, with a studied look of confusion. "It would appear there are very strange happenings near the border of Treglz, though we are quite well-disposed toward Queen Yujur. (*In fact, you would very much like for her to become next Queen of FendrzTreglz and you the king*, Var thought, knowing there was a strong attraction between the two) and her council. I am just now receiving reports of those events and am concerned that perhaps King Hopjur is attempting to insert a wedge of uncertainty between our lands.

"I have taken the liberty to dispatch Dracht to gather information, knowing you were involved in your studies, but it is now becoming serious enough that I feel your particular talents will be needed."

Dracht was Var's closest friend and companion. He was attached to his office as Protector of the Vardan. They spent a great deal of time together, Dracht being interested in the finer arts and Var being fascinated by the free life of the large barbarian warrior.

Dracht had been rescued, as a young child, from a disaster in the Klanx Valley, where a powerful worldshake tremor had caused a flood that had taken his parents. He had grown in the massively muscular form of the barbarians and had shown Var and others that it was not true that the barbarians were of low intelligence. Dracht was "bright," even among the elite in the city. He was also as loyal and honest as anyone Var had ever encountered.

Var nodded solemnly and stated that he had found disturbing signs from that area. There was definitely something wrong there and it had nothing to do with Hopjur. "I fear, My King, that there may be a powerful rogue sorcerer operating in the Sawtooth Mountains – yet I feel that is not the case in the same thought.

"There is, regardless, something wrong there. Very wrong."

Var rose in the stirrups to gaze over the wide pleasant valley below as he came through the cut in the mountains. There was a fog below that seemed a bit out of place for the time of day and he started to wave it away when he stopped.

Perhaps his feelings of ... again, it was purely alienity ... were based in that fog. Dracht was probably down in that valley and dissipating the fog might place him in danger. He would take some caution here, as his natural feelings of being in complete charge of any situation could well be in error. "Move in haste and repent at leisure" was trite, but very true.

There was something different here. There was that odd feeling again. It was a strong feeling that something was not of this place. It wasn't a feeling of evil or even one of impending danger. It was merely something that didn't ... belong. Something, again, alien.

Never forget that a danger unsuspected is a danger unprepared-for.

Var dismounted and removed the carrier from the mount-beast's back, then set a spell to allow the animal to placidly forage while he placed his temporary camp. He was soon comfortable, so started a small fire in the bowl, then took out the focus crystal and asked for the whereabouts of Dracht of it. A picture appeared within it with a very wispy view of a steep rocky ledge with a campsite on it and a large figure moving about. It was indistinct, which meant Dracht, who was surely that figure, was slightly more than twenty four kilometers away, but less than thirty. Closer than twenty four and the picture would become distinct. More than thirty and there would be no response.

Dracht was not moving hurriedly there, so probably was not in any particular danger. Var was sure he would use the emergency call crystal, should that be the case.

Of course, that use would depend on Dracht knowing he was in danger.

Var sighed and turned his attention to the undefined cause of his being there, but found nothing. He used the crystal to quickly view everything ahead for the twenty four kilometers, but all things appeared normal.

Another trite saying: Things are often not as they appear.

That fog was something to consider. It could well be simply a natural thing – there was no feeling of it being a spell – or it could as well be something a very powerful sorcerer brought while hiding the source. If that were the case Var could detect the director of it, but that would entail spells he felt it was wisest not to enjoin here. Not now.

There was still and strongly the nagging feeling that something was not right in this place, but why wasn't the feeling of evil about it? That would seem to be a more natural thing.

Var would study today and would move again on the morrow with the dawn

Cautiously.


Var moved slowly down toward the river that ran through the valley toward the encampment of Dracht. He didn't feel the sense of being watched that had come for a few moments during the night here. Now.

He had placed the "watcher" crystal against the cradle behind the mountbeast's head, but couldn't take the time to use the call spell often. He was moving steadily in the direction of the encampment he'd earlier detected.

There was a large area on the far side of the valley, a more open, very rocky side of a large mountain that had given way when a strong worldshake had shaken it in the time of Var's great grandfather. An indistinct troubling of the dim edges of his consciousness would draw his attention at times, but there was nothing to see that was in any way out of the ordinary – from this great a distance. What would appear as he approached might be very extraordinary. From this vantage, it was merely a rocky, desolate hillside with various plants, cactus-like things, if quite large, growing among the loose rubble.

First, locate Dracht. Don't use the seeker/response spell here. Not until the reason for the sensations were resolved and understood.

Var was in no way afraid for himself. He didn't want to endanger Dracht.

After a little bit more than an hour's travel, Var stopped to use the crystal. Dracht was moving toward the area that Var found to be disturbing. He considered using the response spell to warn Dracht, then decided Dracht had been here for more than ten days already, so was probably in no particularly extreme danger. He was, after all, a very intelligent person.

Var moved on, coming to the river an hour and a half later, where he stopped to eat a bit of the food he carried. There was plenty to eat in the area, so the stores could be replenished before he moved on if he, indeed, did move on. That was yet to be seen.

A quick use of the crystal showed him Dracht was now moving back toward the encampment and that a fog was starting to rise from the river.

Why? The conditions for a natural fog, cool wet air over warm water, did not exist in the middle of the day here. Var could detect no spell that could cause the anomaly. He watched the water carefully, but could see nothing, so stopped to take a sample of the water.

The water was a bit warm. Not to a degree that would be dangerous to fishes or other water life, but much warmer than was natural at this altitude. Something, therefore, was warming the water. The cooler and quite wet air above caused the fog. That part was natural, but was the warmth of the water?

Var rummaged through his case to take out a sparkling opal set on a huge carved diamond in a frame of purest platinum. He concentrated.

There was no spell causing the effect in the river – but there was ... something. Something unnatural.

Someone had detected the use of the crystal. Var sensed the seeker spell and put the crystal away. He would have to forego using seekers and spells until he knew who – or what – was using spells here.

Very strong spells. It was no apprentice. Var did emplace one hider spell. Now only a sorcerer of his strength or more could detect him and his mountbeast. He moved very carefully on toward Dracht's camp.

"Var! Welcome, friend, to my rather boring temporary abode!" Dracht greeted. "What brings you here to the blanklands? Nothing to do at the castle, so you decided to do a little fishing?"

"Fishing isn't my idea of a thing not boring," Var pointed out. "How are things here, my good friend? Any battles to fight or lovely ladies to rescue?"

"I wish!" Dracht replied, laughing. "Then you would have the purpose of rescuing the lovely ladies from me!

"To tell the truth, I know something's wrong, but can't discover what it might be. It's a case where I sometimes see things moving out of the corner of my eye, but there's nothing there when I look directly. I'm watched at night, mostly, but by a spell during the day. You taught me to sense that."

"There is a sorcerer here. He is a powerful one, but that is not what concerns me. There is something else here."

"What?"

"*That*, I can't tell you. Yet," Var answered, drily. "Is there anything you've found here that doesn't seem a likely part of this place? Perhaps a falcon, as some sorcerers can use those birds of prey as information gatherers."

"Nothing I've *seen*. There is something very unnatural here that I've almost seen a number of times. I can feel it watching me and I've used the spells you taught me to learn if a sorcerer was using a watcher spell. Twice there was that, but many more times is was *not* that! It's at the dusk and early dawn when the most such almost-sightings have taken place. Things move at night, but not so close as at those times.

"Would you understand me if I said there was something that wanted to converse with me, but doesn't know how and is afraid?"

"Something? Not someone?" Var asked, watching his friend very closely.

Dracht thought for a moment, then slowly nodded.

"We will find what it is and we will find the sorcerer. I wonder if they are connected, somehow.

"My friend, I think perhaps someone has done an experiment and that experiment did not result in what he was seeking. It is a thing that can happen when one gets careless when an experiment can suddenly – or slowly – become in charge of the experimenter. It is why I have always proceeded with such extreme care. I think a sorcerer has vastly overestimated his own abilities. There is evidence very near here of what his mistake was. It may well be something you have looked at but not seen."

"There are a lot of those! I've gotten some fish and greens and there's bread. I hope you've shown the good sense to bring quality wine, preferably the golden musty-flavored one."

"Yes. I have enough to last for a few days," Var replied, smiling wryly. "One must honor certain conventions, else he is not truly civilized."

"I've never claimed to be civilized," Dracht pointed out. "You're spoiling me with the social conventions stuff. I'll get our supper on the fire. You can set up a comfortable enough bed pack in the tent. I brought the big one ... did you see that?!"

Var cocked his head slightly toward the side.

"Almost. I have sensed it for a few moments. Something glimpsed just to the side. When you look directly there's nothing there. Something seen, as the expression goes, from the corner of the eye."

"I begin to wonder if there are ghosts," Dracht said. "I've never believed in them, but there's something very strange happening here and that's the only explanation I can think of – unless it's just a sorcerer's trick – and you can detect that."

"No. Not a sorcerer's trick, yet yes, that's what it is. It may well be a natural talent of some local animal, but that would hardly get the attention of so many people. The local gentry would know about it to some extent because they would have encountered it. The reports are that there is something of unknown origin."

"Except there aren't any local people here," Dracht pointed out. "There are only a very few travelers who come through the valley and some hunters. There are fishermen who pass on the river, but they don't fish much, here, because the water's too deep and swift for the nets. It was fishermen who first noticed the fog. You saw how it started just past midday and has increased until it's getting dark and yet two hours until the sunset. The times I almost see something is in the fog. By the dawnlight, the only fog here will be natural, but it can be dense. The water's a bit warm here, so cool night air causes natural fog.

"Look who I'm explaining fog to! You *are* known as the Fogmaster of Fendrz!

"Var, my good friend, there's something very wrong here. It's not ghosts."

"No, Dracht. It is not ghosts," Var replied, seriously. "Question is, what *is* it?"

"And is it dangerous?" Dracht finished.

"There is that. Is the water clean enough for bathing? I have ridden astride that mountbeast for nigh on three days and feel I smell it."

"Well, I wasn't going to mention it...." Dracht said, grinning. Var returned the grin and made a common vulgar gesture with his hand and finger.

They went down into the river. The water was comfortable, when it should have been quite cool at that altitude.

"Have you checked the water upstream from here?" Var asked. "Is it so warm all the way to the head of the valley?

"Only to the creek that comes from the east, about three kilometers farther upstream. The creek's quite a lot warmer. I'm planning to search along it on the day past tomorrow. I'm searching a half day away each day and returning here at the twilight. I've been keeping notations, as you've taught me. I'm being thorough and careful."

"I think perhaps we should concentrate on that creek. We know something is not normal there and we can work together. You can supply the brawn and I'll supply the sorcery. Together we should be able to protect each other and to learn something about what we're seeking.

"Dracht, use your peripheral vision. Look at me, but see what is on the bank to your right. If you turn your head it will not be there. It is a natural camouflage, I think."

"Yeah. I've gotten a couple of better glimpses that way, but this is the best," Dracht said, a few moments later. "It seems to be a young boy, but with silvering hair and a beard. He isn't solid-appearing, more like a shadow in the fog. He blends with the fog. It's some kind of ability to change color, I think. He becomes the color of the surroundings and the fog makes him visible if you don't look directly."

"I believe he can change shades of color. He needs the fog because that is more his natural color.

"Dracht, if he wishes to be seen, he will still be there when you look. I will hold him in my peripheral vision to discover if he does totally disappear."

Dracht nodded and turned toward the indistinct figure, which blended into the fog to where it was no longer visible. "I think he can't decide if he wants to be seen or not," Dracht said. "He wants to, but is afraid."

"Green."

"What?"

"He's a very pale green, with the slightest bit of purplish pigment and a little pale yellow," Var answered.

"Which means?"

"I really don't know. Perhaps I'm getting an idea. It is an idea about here – and there."

"You don't make any sense," Dracht accused. "You seldom do."

Var laughed.

Chapter two

Var used the seeker crystal to find who was using the seeker crystal his educated sensibilities detected. There was a quick glimpse of a younger man staring into a crystal from his position in the mouth of a rocky cave, then nothing but the night fog. Var grunted and Dracht asked, "Find anything?"

"There is a sorcerer, quite young, so one with great natural power, sitting in a small cave, using a seeker crystal There is an unusual large rock nearby that looks like the silhouette of a nightstalker cat. He detected my use of the crystal and put out a hiderspell."

"Nightstalker cat? I've seen it. It's no more than six kilometers west above the bend in the river. He's not hiding in a fog shroud?" Dracht asked, smirking. Var shook his head, then nodded.

"Then he doesn't know it's you, I'd guess," Dracht suggested. Var nodded again, then put the crystal away to bring out another one, a bright glowing golden globe on another carved diamond base. He placed fine opals to either side, then energized the globe. He could see a figure in the globe, so concentrated until the figure was quite distinct.

"No one I know. Have you seen him about?"

Dracht studied the figure closely, then said he might have seen him four tenthyears ago when he delivered a gift from Narj to Yujur in Treglz.

"Not in the palace?" Var asked.

"No. He was in the market. The ... herbs and spices stall, if I remember correctly. He was in close conversation with the woman who runs it.

"Var, there was a family resemblance. I did note that, in what you often call 'a subconscious way.' Very distinctive eyes and ears and the same bone structure.

"Do you have any idea how much you affect the way I talk? I sound like an alchemist part of the time and an educated medical practitioner another part. It seems a bit unbarbarian-like to me!"

"Yes. You seem to have managed successfully to combine a more elevated language structure with the barbarian physique. I think you do not object. The combination seems to unduly attract the, as you call them, 'lovely ladies.'

"My friend, I sense we are in terrible danger here while sensing that we are in no danger here. I find that disturbing in the extreme. We are being observed, but *not* by that sorcerer! There is no underlying malice in that watching, but there is no ... understanding. Our watcher finds us strange and doesn't know if we present a danger."

"Do we?"

"Dracht, I don't *know!*" Var cried, with feeling. "There is something very strange here and I do *not* believe it is *of* here! It is here, but not *of* here if you understand what I'm so absolutely unable to say."

"But you know where it *is* of? Are you saying it is something from the demon worlds?"

"Don't call them that. They are other worlds that are this one. We are as much demons to any there as they are to us here. It is my firm belief that they are but other people in other guises and bear no automatic ill will. As strangely,  I don't think that sorcerer bears any malice. I sense he is greatly afraid of what he has done. It is not what was intended. He is young and impetuous and has acted in haste."

"So we'll all repent of his irresponsible actions at our leisure," Dracht finished, dryly.

"I most sincerely hope not. I will set up a warning spell and we will sleep. Tomorrow we investigate a creek."

"It is rather pretty, close to the river here," Var remarked, as he and Dracht moved along the bank of the lazy little creek with the overly warm water. "I wonder if there are merely hot springs that are supplying this creek with the warm water, though none such are known in the area."

"I don't believe so," Dracht replied. "There's usually the odor of sulfur around hot spring water and none here."

Var thought a moment, then removed some dried petals from the red mallow to crush in a small vessel, then added some of the warm water from the creek. The water turned a pale green.

"The water is alkaline while sulfur in the water is acid," Var reported. Dracht was careful to listen to these kinds of things, as he learned so much from Var. "It well could be hot springs, because some are quite alkaline, but I tend to doubt it.

"Dracht, what would warm so much water, other than hot springs? It doesn't make sense."

"I suppose it will when we find the reason. The water's coming from a cave up there. There's also steam coming from the cave."

They approached slowly and Var warned Dracht that something was greatly amiss here. There was a feeling of a portal and not one that, as usually happened, opened for only the seven minutes the spells would maintain.

"Dracht, the spells won't maintain because the area gets *hot* after seven minutes! I think our sorcerer has opened a portal in the water and the water is supposed to make it possible to keep the portal open. I think perhaps our sorcerer now finds he can't *close* the portal now and is deathly afraid for that!"

"So the ones watching us can come and go as they please. They're studying us, as I suppose our sorcerer wanted to do with *them*. Maybe they're not allowing him to come back to close the portal."

"It can be closed from a distance, unless..." Var began, then stopped, thought, and removed the golden globe from his pack and set it up. After almost an hour of careful study he said no one was going through that portal – because it was under the water."

"Then how did they come through to be here now?" Dracht asked.

"We'll have to ask the sorcerer," Var replied, sourly. "We also have to find how many came through and have to learn something of their nature. I sense a watcher is focused on us at the moment, so we will ... *What the...!*" A huge semitransparent face appeared in the mouth of the cave the water was flowing from.

"That's no demon! That's Vardan Kherkth of Gretlz! I saw him at Hop's court on several occasions when you sent me there to investigate the rumors of Hop crossing the border into Fendrz. He seemed able to get Hop's ear with little trouble. I thought he was a minor adviser."

"I've never seen or heard of him. He might be a manipulator, using Hop to his own purposes. He has the power. I've got a blocking spell. He detected my seeker.

"I didn't know there was any sorcerer anywhere with that much power! We must find what he wants here! We have to find the sorcerer at the cave!

"Dracht, I am afraid of nothing in this universe or any other – until now! Something very dangerous is afoot here and that danger could well be for this entire world!"

The two carefully inspected the area. Several times, they felt they were being watched and the seeking face appeared, but Var could easily protect them from the seeking, as it was being maintained from a great distance.

After awhile they went back to the river, then toward the spot where Dracht said the stone image of the nightstalker cat could be found. It was a natural stone that had had some small detail chipped away and was very distinctive for that.

Var kept the hiding spell in place so the young sorcerer would not detect their presence.

They came on the campsite from behind and to the left. The sorcerer was sitting in deep contemplation, thus didn't hear them approach. Var held up a hand and whispered to Dracht that the young man was using a protection spell. There was a seeking, but from a great distance, so it wasn't difficult to remain undetected, though the seeker wielded a very great power. When the sorcerer released the spell Var and Dracht were standing before him. He didn't seem surprised.

"Vardan Herkth, I am Vondar Ricth. People call me Von. I believe we will have many reasons to cooperate closely with what has happened here.

"You will have discovered Vardan Kherkth of Gretlz is our adversary.

"Have you yet met the Lottl?"

"This is Dracht, Von," Var replied. "People call me Var, but that is a common term to describe a sorcerer. You would seem to have far the more power than most students, so why Vondar?"

"I have been forced by events to learn much more than most my age and that has caused much of this, I do not deny. I will brew some stimb and will relate a bit of a story. You will see the necessity of an alliance, but Narjur and Yujur would align without other pressure, I think. There is an obvious deep attraction there and our territories will be joined together before two more cycles if my predictions are correctly found – and they usually are. One needs no talent to see the great attraction between them."

They chatted lightly about palace affairs until the stimb was ready, then sat with it and some sweetbread.

"I will tell you the story now," Von began. "It was about two cycles past when a young student of the spells was taken by his mentor, Vardan Norkht of Velz, to the place we call Nighkt. It was a journey that was to lead to a strange desire to know why he felt such odd sensations of being constantly watched. It was not the sense of danger or evil from such as Vardan Kherkth, but more of a curiosity and confusion state of the watcher, if you understand. Considering that you have been there, you will have felt much the same.

"The student felt – *knew* – there was great intelligence in that observation and as great curiosity and as great difference. It was that difference that so intrigued him.

"The time one may remain in Nighkt is seven minutes, which is not nearly time enough for any real study to be attempted, so the student worked to determine the cause of the failure of the portal spell in seven minutes and found there was great heat at the point of the portal and that the heat caused the spell to cancel itself.

"So. The student felt that, if that heat could be taken away, it would be possible to maintain a portal for much longer, but how could that be accomplished?

"Suffice it to say that much experimentation resulted in the discovery that a slow shower of water would remove the excess heat, thus the portal could remain open for as long as there was energy to direct the spell and that energy could be found easily.

"The student made a spillway from a cool mountain stream to fall against the entrance to the portal, then a simple metal-acid battery could sustain it for many hours. It was then merely necessary to set a falter spell in case something happened to the energy source, in which case the student would have perhaps three minutes to return before the portal failed.

"The student went to Nighkt to explore and discover what the secret of the place may be – and did! He discovered there are people, albeit it very different people, there.

"The people are not greatly different in their physical appearance, yet they may be as they are very capable changelings unless observed from quite close.

"There was a bit of difficulty in exchanging ideas and conversation because the Lottl, for that's what they call themselves, must use many different forms of information exchange than do we.

"The Lottl are, believe it or not, plants! They are changelings and they are plants!

"They are curious and intelligent. Over a period of twelve tenth-cycles the student was able to learn to converse with them and even had helped to move a colony here to Kholworld.

"You understand, they are as curious about us as I am about them. This was a good exchange and all would benefit.

"You see how naive one can be. I felt we could exchange ideas and knowledge and all would live in harmony, as there would be little competition, our basic needs being so radically different. All they need is sufficient rain, and they are almost desert plants, sunlight and moderately rich soil.

"Then, Vardan Kherkth, using a seeker spell to try to discover a way to infiltrate soldiers of his militaristic society into these lands, happened on the portal.

"I was fortunate to be on Kholworld, because he caused the stream to swallow the portal, trapping the Lottl who are here in this place. They cannot go back with the portal under water and I cannot move it.

"Why Kherkth is keeping the portal open, I can't say. I would like to be able to allow my friends to return home, but they are very comfortable here and wish to aid me in ridding this place of such as Vardan Kherkth.

"Perhaps we can, together, find some resolution to these problems? Would you think?"

"We can try," Var answered. "Dracht, have you seen any signs that anyone from Gretlz has traveled here recently in your searches?" Dracht paused, then said, "Directly, no. In the past and through a seeker I would say ... probably.

"I must agree with Von. What's the purpose of keeping that portal open?"

"My friend, what did you say when we first sought after Von?" Var asked. "I believe you will remember saying he didn't know it was me here?"

"A fog shroud as a hider?" Dracht answered, thinking. "Maybe more to the coast, but what good is it here?"

"This is in the wild lands between Fendrz and Treglz. You will note where the river flows."

"To the coast. He can sustain the fogs at this great altitude quite well, but can he sustain them at the coast? To what purpose? What would he want to hide?"

"Var can cause and long sustain a sea fog," Dracht pointed out. "I would imagine that this Kherkth character could. He would want to hide a military force moving between Fendrz and Treglz. He doesn't know about your friends, about the Lottl. I think they're very much at ease in the fog and they can use it far better than Kherkth *OR* us!

"A good time for one of your talents, Var! You can use the fog to our own advantage."

"I wonder," Von said. "I wonder, greatly, if there are already military units moving from the coast up the river. It would seem there are a few too many fishermen lately. There were once no more than a boat every third or fourth day, yet the past tenthcycle there has been at least one per day – and most moving upstream!"

"Then there is an encampment not far from here," Var mused. "We must locate them. We must converse with your friends, the Lottl."

"They don't move very far from their base – I call the plant they are part of the base – because of limits to the amounts of foods they have stored, though they can take their water directly. They prefer the drier rocky places because the roots can be drowned, I think. They are always on the side of a hill, where there is good drainage. The base plant can store water for several tenthcycles and the Lottl can move the plant, if necessary, closer to water, though there is some shock from doing that.

"The colony grows because they take a part of the base to plant elsewhere and at least one of the Lottl will move with that part of the plant. It can grow very rapidly if the soil is rich and the water supply is within certain bounds.

"You can see I have done extensive studies of them.

"I brought the first of the colony here, perhaps eight tenthcycles ago, and they had established four bases when Vardan Kherkth caused the portal to fall into the water. They have established two more bases since. They are aware of everything that happens near the base plant, so will be able to report exactly how many boats have recently moved upstream and how many have moved downstream. Two are positioned where they can observe the river.

"The Lottl are mostly night creatures, but can move about in the fog. They are very good at blending into their surroundings. The base is active and aware in the light and the Lottl at night.

"They do not really understand us and are intelligent enough to know that is not a bad thing and that we will not, cannot, understand them. We can be friends. They do have a code of honor about honesty and loyalty. It is a good code.

"There is enough fog now that we can go to a base, where we can discuss what is happening and, hopefully, make them understand. They do not know war nor deceit, though they know it is part of all animal life and thought. They are intelligent, as I've said. I like them."

"Then we shall try to make an agreement," Var replied. "I predict that there is to be a very difficult time ahead. Kherkth is powerful."

"He is not near. His power is, thus, limited. I do not think he knows about the Lottl. He believes I was attempting to open a bridge to Nighkt, which I was, but he can't know why or what was planned – nor do I know his plan."

"He plans to divide and capture both Fendrz and Gretlz," Dracht said. "If he can establish a large enough camp between them he can send a contingent of ships to the ports in both lands, launch an attack, then have the troops here attack the rear – or the other way around.

"If he can get his soldiers into position here in large enough numbers it would very likely work, but only in the case we didn't suspect. Seeing we know about it, we can spring our own trap."

"Ah, yes!" Var replied. "That largest of all words, 'if'! The barbarian mind is expert in such matters. You, my friend, can have the troops of both Fendrz and Gretlz ready and Von and I will engage this sorcerer. We can defeat him if we force things to be in our time, not his.

"Von, shall we go to meet the Lottl? I find them quite fascinating, already, and have but fleetingly glimpsed one or two of them in a fog!

"Tell me, what the names plants use like? Very different from our own?"

"They don't have individual names and the communicate in some fashion I can't fathom among themselves," Von answered. "I simply call them 'Base One,' 'Base Two' and so forth."


"One, this is Vardan Herkth. We call him Var," Von introduced. Var and Dracht felt a bit silly being introduced to a plant – a large cactus, by the look. "This is his friend and companion, Dracht. They wish to know the Lottl and to learn what you may have gathered about the movement of boats on the river. I give you my bond that they are friends and wish you no harm." Von had a seeker crystal before him that Var immediately understood was the only way to speak with an unlike being in a language he couldn't understand.

A foggy shape stepped from what was a large shoot a moment before and studied Var and Dracht with an old, bearded face on a lad's body. It made a few signs, then a wispy voice that seemed to come from the air above them said, "I represent One. How may we aid you and to what end?"

Von said, "There is a plot of some kind being ordered by Vardan Khekth, who has blocked the portal. We believe he intends instigating a military action against Fendrz and Treglz at once. He has caused troops to be sent to the near area to either begin an attack on both countries at once or to attack after other troops attack the major port cities of both countries."

"To what possible purpose? Would he not then become responsible for both of these places? Would not that responsibility be one that a reasonable sane being would wish to avoid?" One asked, clearly confused.

"No. That's not the way they think," Dracht answered. "He wants power."

"With power comes more responsibility," One pointed out. "Thus it would seem far the more intelligent course to disperse that power, thus the responsibility, to others who are far more qualified to administer – that is the word you used, my friend? – justice and to give aid where needed. It would seem garnering of such power would have little or no real advantage, would, indeed, offer much disadvantage.

"We will aid you, of course, though we fail to understand these things. What would you have us do?"

"Are your bases found only here in the rocky slopes?" Var asked. "Are there any at a height to observe past the river to the north?"

Von explained "north" to One, who said there were only the four colonies and they were quite close. It understood there was suitable land in many places in this part of Kholworld and it could establish as many colonies as might prove necessary in those places. The colonies could not thrive in wetter areas than this, but could do well in more desert-like areas.

"You can observe fire from a distance?" Dracht suddenly asked and One agreed that the colony could detect fire in many ways, both observation and smell being the more important ones. There were small fires to the north.

"How far? Can you tell?" Dracht asked. That led to Von, Var and Dracht having to explain both of those expressions, "How far" meaning "At what approximate distance away" and "tell" meaning "discern." One made a joke about the inexactitude of language and Dracht and Var both decided they liked it. A shared sense of humor was a bonding.

The troops were perhaps thirty or forty kilometers to the north-northeast. There were probably two groups of them, as there were two locations of the small fires.

They talked about various things and learned much about each other. Var said the lands each utilized were so far different in characteristics that there would never be a conflict. What the Lottl needed was very much what Kholians had no use for and vice versa. One was soon joined by a representative of Two, then by Three and Four. They made plans to meet again when there was a purpose to it. The things they had to know now were things they would have to discover for themselves. Var promised he would speak with Queen Yujur and King Narjur about welcoming the Lottl to those areas where they would flourish. One said the Lottl would produce seed that could be taken to those places, along with a piece of the base plant to watch over them as they matured.

"You know something, Var?" Dracht said as they walked back toward their campsite in the company of the Lottl and Von, "I think we can probably work very well together with the Lottl in protecting this land for all time!

"I have been to the barbarian lands and have a little influence there. There are plenty of places in the lands where the Lottl will be comfortable.

"Yes, I think, just maybe, I have an idea or two!"

"We fare well with the barbarians in Melgrd," Von said. "They are often in the border towns to trade. The only real difference in them and us is that they do not like cities and what we call civilization and we do not like the unstructured and hard life they lead.

"As Mother says, we are bred to ease, they are bred to hardship. One does only that which his ancestry dictates."

"Not only me," One replied. "All do. It is what, as you say, ancestry dictates."

That led to a few jokes about words. "One mustn't speak of what one does when One is present," Von declared. "That leads to one large confusion!"

"It has done that!" One agreed.

The mood was lighter as they entered the campsite. They talked and got to know one another until late in the night. Von walked back to his camp with Two. One, Three and Four went back to their base plants (The Lottl could "see" perfectly in the dark, much better than in the light) and Var and Dracht slept until past the dawn.

"My friend, we will have to go to the north to observe the camps of Khekth's soldiers," Var stated, "I wonder if it were best we first do something about the portal."

"If you do something about the portal, Khekth's going to know you're here," Dracht pointed out. "Von and the Lottl can keep him occupied while we're away. Better he doesn't suspect we're onto his schemes.

"Var, are we going to have to fight two large contingents of warriors by ourselves, here? Von can help a bit, but the Lottl will be useless in a fight. Their nature is to hide, not to confront, and we can't get soldiers from Fendrz or Treglz. What few they have will have to stay to defend if there's an attack at the ports. There isn't time to train an army, anyhow.

"I think we're in some deep trouble here!"

"We will borrow a trick or two from the Lottl," Var replied. "It's not easy to defeat an invisible foe. We are going to blend into our surroundings and remain unseen. That will add the fear of the unknown to our arsenal.

"My friend, we're going to be only two people fighting a war for two countries – and they may never know about it.

"We have one more advantage, and it is a large one."

"What's that?" Dracht asked, grinning.

"You," Var answered, returning the grin.

Chapter three

The first consideration will be to manufacture a strategy that has a hope of working and it must be one that includes elements to allow a vardan, a vondar and a barbarian – plus a number of strange plant/people to defeat a large army and a very powerful vardan.

That might well prove an insurmountable task.

Unless one makes the attempt, one can never know the potential of a plan!

"Dracht, we will be forced to use the tactics of our foe against him," Var warned. "Kherkth is, in what I feel to be a great stroke of exceptional good fortune for us, using a device about which I am somewhat knowledgeable. I think perhaps fog as a shield against discovery was not among the wisest of choices."

"Well, consider that he probably doesn't know that's your main strength," Dracht pointed out, turning the dawnmeal cakes. "It is in our favor.

"We have another thing he's using that we can probably use to a better advantage than he can."

Var waited a moment, then asked, "And that is?"

"Divide and defea. It's second nature to a barbarian, of which I am one, so he's left attacking not one, but two of our strengths."

"Which would tend to indicate he doesn't know our weaknesses, yes. We have a very good place to begin our campaign, in that he has chosen to construct two separate encampments. That places his forces into the positions into which he planned to place Fendrz and Treglz."

"It does?" Dracht answered, a bit surprised, then he grinned and agreed, "It *does!*"

"We will have to observe these military encampments while remaining unobserved, ourselves," Var cautioned. "I wonder how we can ... there is no watching spell he can't detect even from a great distance, as it cannot be a small thing when concerned with more than a very few and an army of very few against two large areas is doomed before the first arrow flies.

"We can use the fog, certainly, but I suspect the camps will be placed above the river fogs, thus any unexplained occurrence would likely be immediately noted and would as immediately be investigated."

Dracht nodded, then asked, "How long before the season of rains?"

"A tenthcycle or less. Why?"

"Because there are very natural fogs then that you can simply make stronger."

Var thought, nodded, sighed and said he had a small idea forming. Call it an idea emerging from a fog.

"What will you do?" Von asked. "It is almost the tenth-cycle before the rains begin."

"You know that. Dracht knows that. The Lottl know that. I know that. Everyone who resides in the whole area knows that," Var replied, smugly. "But Vardan Khekth does *not* know that! He has nothing more than second-person reports upon which to base his actions!

"I predict there will be a very light rain today higher in the mountains that will supply enough moisture in the air to bring about a heavy fog that rolls down the mountainside during the night to encompass those camps.

"Von, I will require your help in bringing that rain and we will be exhausted on the morrow, as it will certainly be no small task to bring that much moisture from a distance. It will be rather difficult to do so in a way that Khekth will not note, but the Lottl will have the fog to be able to move about and gather what information we will need and Dracht will be able to be awake and aware in the morning to direct the efforts. I will have the strength to hold the fog in the camps for perhaps an hour at the dawning."

"For what?" Dracht replied. "The Lottl will be able to work better during the night than after the dawn."

"Ah! But you *won't*!" Var said, smirking. "It will serve us well to introduce a bit of 'That was a strange thing to happen!' among those soldiers, don't you think? We won't wish to do anything that might cause them to fear more than a nagging wonder about the unknown."

"Can't the Lottl do that?" Von asked.

"*No*! I do not consider it would be to anyone's advantage for the Lottl to be asked to do anything more than to observe! They are not warlike nor violent and have no understanding of what we are doing or why we do it. This is not their greed nor is it their fight. It is our inherent responsibility."

"I don't have any vaguest notion what you plan or what it'll accomplish," Dracht replied. "I'm willing to try whatever you think will work.

"What's the plan?"

"Here's what we'll first attempt to do," Var confided, conspirationally. "First, the Lottl. They will count the personnel and the weapons and note the types. They will note several things as to food supplies and so forth and the ways being prepared to move large numbers of people across the mountains and in which directions. I believe one camp will move against Fendrz and the other against Treglz.

"The Lottl will be able to do that in a short time before the dawnlight and will be able to return to their bases.

"Dracht, you can go into one of the camps at dawnlight. The kinds of things you will do....

Captain Hacz of the Gretlz 1st Regiment looked a bit askew at the private who had come to report something strange.

"What is this manure you men are spreading about a ghost in the armory?" he demanded. "So there was a heavy fog, and some things got misplaced! All we have to do is tighten up on discipline!"

"Sir! The men say the fog wasn't natural, and that things were moved after they were properly placed and inventoried, as is the requirement!" Private Fulnc replied, stiffly. "I mean, Sir!, that something is not *right* here!"

"For the screech of a blackcawer!" Hacz snarled. "We all saw there was a rainstorm just at dusk higher in the mountains! When there's a rain up high, the fog comes down the mountain because the ground the rain fell on is warm, so it's the same as the fog when the river's warmer than the air! That's why we were able to come here without anyone seeing us! Vardan Khekth used a perfectly natural weather condition by causing the water to be warm. That's all!

"You *did* hear that? A perfectly *natural* kind of weather condition?

"So! That part's explained, even though an idiot should be able to figure it out without further explanation!

"Now, what's this about things moving?"

"Sir! The crossbows and shields were put in the racks after practice, according to regs! Sergeant Andjc wrote the inventory before the doors were closed and barred for the night. Privates Donj and Gleflt stayed, as per orders, awake and alert the entire guard shift and all items were still in place when their shift was completed.

"When Sergeant Andjc went in to sign out the items to the troops they were all jumbled together on the conference and strategy table, Sir!"

"All? All the shields and all the crossbows? Not *some* of them?"

"*All*, yes Sir! Also all the crossbow bolts, Sir!"

"The room was never without a guard?"

"No Sir! The shift change and exchange of inventory and the duty ledgers was completed in the anteroom, as is procedure! The only time there was no one inside the gear room itself was then and the three guards and the disbursement officer were in the anteroom with full view of the only door the entire time, which was no more than the quarter hour."

"So they send you, a mere private, to report?" Hacz said, with a questioning sneer.

"Yes, Sir! They called me to report it to you immediately, as they did not wish to leave the post until there is an explanation, Sir!"

"Well, they did that part of it right, at the least" Hacz mumbled. "Dismissed! Tell Andjc I'll be over there in a few minutes. I'm quite sure there's some easy and simple explanation – but one that doesn't leave them in a good position!"

"Sir!" Fulnc replied, spun and left.

*What the nine hells now*? Hacz wondered.


"I managed to leave them with a small puzzle," Dracht reported. "What did you learn from the Lottl?"

"Two hundred four soldiers at the north camp and three hundred nine at the east camp," Var replied. "They have armaments in the usual proportions and food enough for at least a tenthcycle. The east camp is clearing a roadway to the Glangel Valley into Fendrz and the north is clearing a roadway into Treglz.

"We wait one day, then give the other camp a puzzle of some kind. I want to make them nervous, but not to particularly scare them – yet. I have to keep this on a level where Khekth can't detect what I'm doing."

"He'll have to come here to learn anything?"

"Exactly. I can't hope to fight him successfully from this distance and know how to get him to come here, but will want his soldiers demoralized enough by the time he comes that they will prove useless to him.

"I've arranged with Von to keep the puzzles going after three days with small but strange happenings."

"After three days?"

"We will be visiting Queen Yujur, then Narj, before we return here to lure Khekth into the trap he is making. I'll wish to spend the morrow in an investigation of the river below this point."

Dracht thought a moment, then nodded.


"This is better than I had hoped," Var noted to Dracht. "The river is quite narrow here and there is a close enough and high enough rocky embankment with protection to allow us to fairly well stop anymore soldiers coming here."

"The current's strong," Dracht noted in turn. "We can make them withdraw the oars and they will not be able to stay close. We can remove the pullrope and they can't hope to fight it.

"I worry that the legitimate fishermen won't be able to use the river, either."

"We can use cords to raise the pullrope up when it is not fishermen who need to use it. There will then be no need for concern. There is good chance we will not use the river approach plan. Khekth will surely know troops here are not defensible. Once he is aware we know of his plans this will not be again used. He can resist attack by us or he can resist the nature of the river currents. He cannot resist both and will be aware of that.

"Very well. We will go back to the area of the encampments for you to increase the uncertainty among the soldiers, then we will go to Treglz."

"My friend, I begin to believe I have more to offer here than mere bravado. I had hoped to discourage Khekth's adventurism, but I now feel we may be able to defeat him."

"It is not a sure thing and is not an easy thing."

"Few things in life are."


"Queen Yujur, I bring you greetings from King Narjur," Var said. "I have been working on a project in the Sawteeth Mountains and needed to come here for information. I would speak with Vardan Fekth. It is a matter of great import for both Fendrz and Treglz, I fear. There is a danger that must be addressed."

"I have felt there is something amiss, Var. There are many strange reports from the mountain people.

"Dracht, welcome. It is always a pleasure."

"Thank you, Your Highness, I always feel very welcome here. It is always a pleasure for me to be here in this city and in your presence. You are and always have been a perfect hostess."

"Thank you. You, as always, say the perfect thing. Perhaps we may gossip a bit while the vardans discuss their business," she said, smiling. "I have said before that I do not like to spread gossip, but there isn't much else one can do with it!"

They strolled off to enjoy refreshments and chat and Var headed for Vardan Fekth's study. He met Captain Wlad, head of Queen Yujur's palace guard, and stopped to discuss using a contingent of soldiers in the Sawteeth Mountains to prevent an infiltration.

"Infiltration? By whom?" Wlad asked.

"Minions of Vardan Khekth of Gretlz."

"I've long warned about that one! He's too ambitious! I've often said that!

"Have you discovered anything upon which to base your beliefs?"

"More than five hundred soldiers are already encamped in the mountains. I've seen them, directly."

"Yes. If they are not expected, they could wreak havoc on this kingdom. Do you have a plan?"

"In an early formative stage, yes. I'll wish to discuss some things with Fekth."

"Vardan Herkth, I'm afraid Fekth has never had much personal power, though he is certainly very intelligent in science. It's probable that I can be of much more aid than can he, in these rare situations.

"There is an apprentice called Vondar Ricth who would seem to have more real power in the arts than anyone I've known of in my life, short of yourself. His mother has some power, using medical arts and herbs."

"Yes. I agree. I've met him and he is working with me."

"Ah! Then complete victory is assured! Khekth cannot stand against the two of you! He doesn't have that much power!"

"I wish I were half as certain of that as are you, my friend."


"Greetings, Fekth! I hope you are well?" Var said, when Fekth opened the door to the study.

"Ah! Do come on in, Herkth. I've just been trying to discover why magnetite attracts iron, as there is no spell about it. It is a natural thing.

"Why does one side pull another piece of magnetite strongly and the other repulse it? What manner of science allows that?

"It isn't your interest, but it fascinates me."

"It is an interest and I agree there is no spell concerned," Var replied. "I cannot prevent or cause it, but have noted some interesting things about it.

"I know you have done some studies with the gas released when acids are poured on limestone. I understand it can make a fire go out and that it can cause a person to become unconscious, or even to die?"

"It seems to be the same gas that a wood fire produces," Fekth lectured, brightening at a discussion of something he had studied carefully. "I have heated limestone to where it glows and falls into the powder that can burn the skin if water is added. It gives off the same gas and, when dissolved in water, with the gas very concentrated, and mixed into the water, will again form limestone!

"Did you know that the breath, when blown through the limestone residue in water, will also form limestone? The gas from a wood fire will also form limestone?

"It is a fascinating study! I learn these things, but can't discover *why*! The air we breath in when passed through the solution will form *some* small bit, but the breath when we breath *out* will form substantially more.

"I theorize the body somehow produces that gas and breathing allows its release. If it is allowed to build to a certain level, it can kill and this gets it out.

"I connect firewood with food. Somehow, our body actually burns the food, producing the gas.

"Now, we burn wood for energy. It is fuel for the fire. Isn't it, therefore, logical that the body burns food for energy? The burning produces the same gas?"

"Fekth, I have often said you are brilliant. You may have made a very important discovery! We have a situation where I may need a large reservoir of that gas. Is there a way to concentrate it in a large area?"

"Well, I have noted that it tends to go down and will concentrate most in the lowest spot. Over a very large area, I think not. It *is* part of the air and will mix and dilute."

"Do you only need a gas that will cause many people in a large area to become unconscious?"

"That's mostly what I need."

"I think I can help you there, but you must understand that it will probably also render *you* unconscious, if you use it. I've found that some very easy gases to produce will do it. I know you've heard of ether, a form of alcohol, if my studies are correct."

"Yes. It will tend to explode, which may well become what we're forced to do, though I really haven't the hardness of psyche to wish harm to people who may be, for the most part, innocent."

"All you have to do is be certain it is not used around a fire."

"But the place I would have to use it has quite a number of fires."

"Then you would not be interested in the gas from the Grimmith root. It kills. Very quickly. Heat will render it unnatured and harmless.

"If you are speaking of a large concentration of people you merely wish to render unconscious, you can use any number of things in the water or food. It is a matter of seeing that they all partake. Some of them work quickly, some take a few minutes."

"Ah! And an army eats together at almost the same time and we need not concern ourselves if only a few do not lose consciousness! You are brilliant, my friend!"

"An army eats together? Then what I've heard of the mountains is true? There is an army gathering there?" Fekth asked.

"Yes. Where did you hear it?"

"I don't really remember. I think some mountain people came to town for supplies. We chat about things when I'm in the square."

Var shook his head and grinned. Most people would immediately run to Queen Yujur with that kind of information. It was the luck of the game that the people who talked about it chose Fekth, who would certainly consider it something the queen would know about, not realizing that the mountain folk wouldn't speak with the queen and wouldn't trust the guard.

Fekth looked quizzically at Herkth and asked, "Is there a danger from them? Here? I should have carried the words to Yu?"

"There is danger, but I don't think Queen Yujur could do anything. Perhaps Captain Wlad, but that might not end too well, either. He wouldn't suspect the extent of the danger.

"Well, it's a problem I have to work out."

"Herkth, I have an old book about going to other worlds, such as Nighkt, that was written by Vardan Joikth more than four hundred years ago. If I remember, he went to many worlds and one of them, when the portal was opened, had a cold wind blow out that put out the fires in the area and caused several people very close by to become unconscious and one to die. He developed a sudden strong headache and was nearly unconscious himself when he closed the portal. He was above the others, so wasn't as quickly affected, I believe.

"I had not thought of that book in years! I wonder! Was that the fire gas? The gas from the limestone?"

"Was the pattern described in the book?!" Var asked, becoming excited.

"Oh, yes. All of them. Let me see ... not that one ... it had a blue thread holding it ... *ah!*"

He slipped a book from the shelf and placed it on the table. "It was toward the front section, if I remember."

"It's in code!" Var pointed out.

"Hmm? Oh, yes. I can read it. It's a simple numbers code and they are always easy," Fekth said, as he opened the book.

Chapter four

"You can open a portal above each of the camps," Von suggested. "It is an easy spell and configuration. I think we can be sure it is not a fatal thing if we limit the time it is in use to only a few minutes. It has been noted that stopping breathing will cause unconsciousness in only a minute or two and death in most after perhaps five minutes, barring other damage.

"I can't understand why you feel we should wait to do it, though. It would seem wisest to simply remove the effectiveness of the soldiers as quickly as possible."

"I'll want to close the portal to cause Khekth to come here. He must be dealt with or ending this adventure will merely begin his next against us. We cannot stop him in Gretlz. It is, in a manner of speaking, the pool he dug, so he well knows the depths of."

"Ah, yes! We say the barn he has built," Von agreed. "I imagine he will come here, but is it wise that those soldiers be awaiting his arrival?"

"We take care of that bunch after he's almost here," Dracht said. "Let him think he has the protection until he enters the trap. We'll just have to be sure there isn't a hole in the trap or a back exit we don't know about.

"Var, I think we can do something that will give us the best chance against him and his soldiers.

"Can you be cetain the gas from the portal won't harm the Lottl? They won't be able to move out of its path easily."

"We'll have to work with them," Var agreed.

"One, we don't know how the gas from a fire affects your people and don't wish to do anything to endanger you," Von explained. "I know that some things that are good for plants are deadly to animals and vice versa.

"Do you understand what I'm asking?"

"Do you mean close to the fire or more at a distance?" One asked in reply.

"Just the gas, not the heat," Var said.

"I don't understand. It is very much something we need, if you mean the gas that ... ah! I understand!

"My friends, that is a thing we have much studied because we have noted in long history that it is the critical link between our people and animals! My people use that gas to survive and release the gas that causes things to burn more intensely, while animals use the gas we release to survive and release the gas we need in a never-ending cycle. It is what we call the life-link cycle.

"Have no fear that the gas will harm us. Quite the opposite! It increases our health!"

"Then all we have to do is somehow prove it's the same gas," Dracht warned. "To this point, it's only that it *seems* to be the same gas."

"Maybe we can open a small portal and let One test it, if there is a way?" Von suggested.

"I cannot, as it is a thing that needs light to activate and my place is not in the light, but home can detect it very accurately."

They discussed various gases as they went to the Base One plant, where they had a long and careful discussion. Base One had Var open a very small portal close to a branch. It said the gas was quite cold, but was, indeed, the gas from fires.

"Then it's a matter of outsmarting Khekth, it seems," Dracht said. "Now I'll tell you my plan! I think it would be a bad move to underestimate Vardan Khekth. We can't hand him a victory because we did that."

"We will close the portal," Var decided. "I can detect when he approaches because he will use a seeker spell."

"I think he has already used a communication spell and learned of the fogs and things moved," Von said. "One has told me about the way the soldiers are acting and says there is some kind of device being constructed that sounds very much like a thing to detect invisible intruders.

"As One watched them build it, he was able to avoid sounding a warning."

"Ah! I *thought* I had detected a slightly changed position in the last seeker Khekth sent!" Var cried. "My friends, he is already on his way here! Shall we prepare his greeting?"

It would take a fast ship five days to cross the ocean from Gretlz. They would be ready.

It was a bit less than a day until Khekth should arrive. Dusk was falling as Var and Von opened their portals above the encampments. They kept the gases from coming until the lantern lights were lowered for the sleep period, then allowed the gases to flow down the mountainside into the camps until all the fires were extinguished. Var, Von and Dracht went into the camps when the gases had moved on down the mountain after the portals were closed and removed the weapons. It was easy for the sorcerers to keep the soldiers asleep where they couldn't have put so many to sleep at once. A couple of mountbeasts and carts and the weapons were gone when the soldiers awakened in the morning.

Var, Von, Dracht, One and Two were sitting around their own campfire while Var used a seeker to find Khekth. He was last noted near the mouth of the river into the sea just before they went on their raid of the encampments.

"It would seem he suspects something," Var finally said. "He isn't using any spells.

"Well, we can position ourselves and Wlad's men at the narrows on the river and trap him when he comes upstream."

"Wlad's men?" Von asked.

"Yes. I sent the message for him to send fifty good men this morn," Var replied. "We made that arrangement when Dracht and I were in Treglz. We will have quite a surprise for that boat, when it comes!"

"Well, what now?" Dracht asked the following afternoon. "Two boats of fishermen, four persons per boat. No soldiers no Khekth."

"Hoo-ooo-ooo!" came from a bit downstream. "It would seem you spoke one minute too soon!" Von said, grinning. "That's the signal that Wlad's men have spotted the boat!"

Var moved quickly to the rocks to watch as the boat rounded the rocky point into the river. It was a typical shallow water warship with about twenty soldiers aboard. They were  hauling the boat along, using the rope. It was extremely hard labor to pull such a vessel against that current.

Var signaled for Wlad's soldiers to take their positions and stood on the rock outcrop. He was immediately seen by the soldiers on the boat, but they didn't offer him any challenge.

"Vardan Khekth! Show yourself!" Var called. "You are anticipated here!"

"He ain't on this boat!" came back. "He done come up eventide last! He ain't with you guys?"

"He thinks we're Khekth's soldiers!" Dracht hissed. "The rocktoad came up in one of those fishing boats!"

"Release the rope and go back to Gretlz or perish here!" Var called. "You will not be given another chance!"

"What..?! Who..?!" the soldier yelled. "You ain't tellin' me what to do!"

Wlad's men stood and moved closer to the water, many crossbows cocked and ready.

"You were saying?" Var called. "Release the rope and go back! Now!"

The boat was exposed while the soldiers on the bank had cover in the rocks. The captain saw his chances were nil and threw up his hands. The boat began to move downstream. Wlad's soldiers pulled the ropes higher than the boatmen could reach. The intruders could no longer use them again.

"It seems Khekth did manage to outsmart us," Dracht said dryly. "What now?"

"Khekth didn't outsmart us, we outsmarted ourselves," Var said. "Well, he has an army, but no arms. Wlad's men can capture them, but will have to wait, because I don't wish to send them into a trap. Khekth is powerful and has no least compunction against using methods that would kill all of them.

"It seems this will soon become a deadly battle between vardans. Khekth will not willingly take leave of his power, so this will become a war to the death of at least one of us."

"You thought about one other thing?" Dracht asked.

"What?" Var returned sourly.

"Defeating Khekth will result in the necessity of you taking full charge over Gretlz. Those *are* Hopjur's soldiers there. Despite the fact it is Khekth's scheme, it is Gretlz who has attacked Fendrz and Treglz!"

Var swore, colorfully. *Very* colorfully!

They left two watchers with a call crystal to watch the river, then headed back toward the invaders' encampments with the rest of Wlad's troops. They met no resistance, as the soldiers knew full well a fight with no weapons against even such a smaller well-armed force would be hopeless. Wlad would march them to Treglz, where they would be put on ships and sent home. Wlad and others questioned that action, but Queen Yujur agreed with Var, Dracht and Von that reparations against soldiers conscripted against their will and sent to attack a country they held no personal animosity toward would inevitably result in that animosity forming and nothing else. It would also be a strong warning to Hopjur.

That handled, Var and Dracht went back to their own little camp in the mountains. Queen Yujur asked why they would go there instead of back to Fendrz.

"Because Vardan Khekth, the schemer who would make such a plan to attack these lands, is still there, somewhere," Dracht replied. "He is still exactly the threat to the security of our lands as he was two days past. If he returns to Gretlz it will be only a matter of time until he designs another plan to seize power over others and that next one might not be so easy to thwart.

"It will be to us – to Var, anyhow – to see that does *not* happen!"

"Well, my friend, this might well become a contest we will not win," Var warned. "Khekth is a very intelligent and powerful foe."

"Nah. He's a clever and cunning foe, not an intelligent one," Dracht replied. "There comes Von. I wondered that he might not join us in this battle.

"Now, *there* is your intelligence!"

"With that, I must agree most fully!" Var returned. "Von! I would welcome you back to our humble abode, if you can call a tattered old tent and a campfire an abode."

"It suffices to fill the definition. Treglz was attacked. How could you doubt I would come to aid in finding and destroying the attacker?"

"I didn't doubt it, even expected you to come, if not quite so soon," Var said. "I felt you would await the departure of the Gretlz contingent.

"You have considered that Khekth may have emplaced a plan of resistance and rebellion, in the case where they were captured?"

"Very certainly!" Von answered, with a wry grimace. "It is why I instructed Wlad and his troops to befriend them and to make jokes."

"Make jokes?"Dracht asked, surprised. "Now *that* was a stroke of brilliance! When men are able to laugh together they will not attack those who share the humor.

"I rather tend to seriously doubt Khekth will have considered that little fact in his training!"

"I tend to seriously doubt that Khekth *has* a sense of humor," Var agreed. "We must find him and a way to render him impotent in his power. That is no small task — either phase."

"Oh, I think we can find him, very easily," Von replied. "Are you forgetting we have allies, even here? Allies he has no idea even exist? Allies who can watch his every move?"

"Ah! The Lottl!" Dracht said, smugly. "It isn't easy to beware of an enemy one doesn't know exists, can't see and can't understand."

"But there is no more fog since I closed the portal," Var pointed out.

"There is still night," Von returned.


"One, do you know where any who were not taken by the army to Treglz are hiding?" Von asked.

"I am Three," the being who had come to the campsite at dusk answered. "There are none."

"*None?!*" Dracht cried. "That *cannot* be!"

"Did any go farther up the river?" Von asked.

"No, but a small boat with but two passengers did go down the river perhaps a moment before your soldiers came to the camps," Three replied.

"Well, we were outsmarted, that time!" Var declared. He took out a glowing crystal in a base made of pearls taken from the large clams in the bay at Downsouth. He used it to check with the two soldiers watching the river, told them to lower the ropes so the fishermen could use them and asked if any boats had gone downriver since Wlad's soldiers had gone to the camps.

No?

A slow and almost evil grin spread across Var's face. "It would seem that Khekth has once again outsmarted himself!" he stated positively.

"Var, tell those soldiers to lower the rope, but to remain at their positions. Khekth may wait until they leave to go downriver."

Var gave the instructions, then put the caller crystal away. "He has already gone downriver. He is playing a game of yes-no."

Yes-no was a game that used a two-possibility situation, such as the flipping of a coin, to decide a winner. If it was a matter of figuring whether a person would answer yes or no to a question it was no longer a half-half chance, because one could use personality factors to deduce what an answer would be under a given circumstance.

"Ah, yes! Being cunning and clever!" Dracht agreed. "Leave the boat and go on foot around the guards. It is our misfortune that the far side of the river is so damp and shaded or the Lottl would have seen him."

"That should be easy enough to learn," Von suggested. "Shall we seek along the river for the boat?"

"Yes, but not with a seeker spell," Var replied. "He can detect a spell and will know we are aware of his trickery."

"We can use a bit of trickery, ourselves! Two teams make the game!" Dracht said. "I can use a boat, we can go downriver in it and you can detect if *he* uses a seeker spell to watch us."

"But he wouldn't know we were doing that," Von pointed out.

"Unless he did *not* go past the guards by a land route downriver?" Var asked. "My friend, that strategy can answer two questions at one cast!

"Where do we find your boat?"

"We can use one that was being used at an encampment," Dracht answered. "It is a matter of changing a few superficial things about it to make it hard to recognize from a distance. The boats are very much alike that are used on the river, so there will be no way to know it is a vessel from there."

"Unless he has a spell on the boats, but we can detect that – and use it!" Von agreed. They moved toward the camp landings.

They selected a rather ordinary boat and Var produced a pigment from the stickysap tree that changed the color from a dull gray to a pale green that the local fishermen used. They dressed in fishermen's cloaks and shade-hats and drifted downstream with only an occasional minor bit of steering with the oars and rudder. They found a boat drawn into a small cove with overhanging weeper trees. Von said there was a contact spell on the boat as they approached.

"Ah!" Dracht said, smugly. "He is still in the area and intends to come back for the boat!"

"Yes. There would be little purpose in leaving the spell if the boat was meant to be permanently abandoned," Von agreed. "That means he did not move past the guards downstream."

"I wonder! Perhaps he ... I think I must risk a seeker spell!"

"He will certainly know you are seeking him. It will not be unexpected."

"But he will not know if it is something else I seek."

"Such as a large boat full of soldiers?" Dracht asked. "Armed soldiers?

"It is what I might do, had I expected to find a guard against them. Let them seem to retreat, but wait in a place where I could march *them* around the guard point above the river!

"What can he do with those few soldiers, well-armed or no?"

"Well-armed, few – and *unexpected!*" Var corrected. "Remember what we were able to do against two full camps of well-armed soldiers because we were unexpected?"

"They are useless if expected," Dracht said. "My friend, I feel Khekth is a coward and will not be with them."

"True, perhaps, but he will be with that boat soon enough!" Var replied. "The unexpected is only effective when it is."

"Is?" Von asked.

"Unexpected," Dracht replied.

"They will move soon after darkness, using the starlight to find their way," Von decided. "It is bright this time of the year and the ground is not difficult to traverse."

"Wouldn't it be terrible if a sudden dense fog were to move down the mountainside?" Var wondered. "Wouldn't it be ... unexpected? Wouldn't it be beyond belief that anyone around here could produce such a phenomenon at all?"

"They would light torches," Von said.

"And become visible for that," Dracht added.

"It wouldn't matter, because they would be immediately ineffective as a force," Var noted. "Such are the vagaries of fate.

"Von, can you hold a hider ... no. We have to do something and I can't think of a way," Var continued. "I want to do something to that boat, but the contact spell will prevent it, I'm afraid, because he will instantly know something was done."

"What do you wish done?" Von asked.

"I want to put a thing in place that will allow the boat to move into the river, then begin rapidly taking on water," Var answered.

"That should be no real problem," Von said.

"Because?" Dracht asked.

"Because the particular contact spell doesn't report anything if a plant does something to the boat," Von replied, this time with a smug look of his own. Both Dracht and Var matched the expression.

"Ah! And Khekth will run for that boat, first business, when his soldiers are lost to him – because he's a coward!" Dracht said. "*This* is a favor we should not feel reticent to ask of the Lottl. It exposes them to no danger."

Von said he would speak with the Lottl and would have careful instructions for them.


"Ah! Here they come!" Dracht said. "The fog is just becoming visible above them from here and they will be in it in perhaps three or four minutes. We will use the voice displacement spell to convince them they are surrounded and they can't know if it's true or not!"

"The boat will be ready for Khekth," Von said. "Two and One have done as you asked and the plug is held with a vine that will allow the boat to move into the current before it is pulled. The motion of the boat in the current will ensure that the plug will not long remain in the boat to be replaced."

They waited until the soldiers had moved very slowly and cautiously (and very nervously) into the fog for Dracht to shout, "Halt! We have you surrounded and we can see you! Lay down your weapons and place your hands on top of your heads! There will be no second warning!"

"Post two reporting subjects in sight!" Von shouted from about a hundred meters farther ahead, then Von from behind and on the far side from Dracht, then voices, seemingly hundreds of them, rang out reporting positions all around the area.

There was a confused clatter as weapons were dropped. The fog slowly weakened until the forms of the closer soldiers could be seen as silhouettes. There were many other silhouettes surrounding them. They were herded to a central area and told to sit on the rocks and await orders. Dracht, Var and Von collected the weapons in a cart and hauled them away.

"I knew about the voice displacement, but how did you work the other soldiers with us?" Dracht asked Var.

"I have no knowledge of how that was done," Var answered. "I imagine it was you, Von?"

"No," Von replied. "I thought it was you."

A Lottl was suddenly walking with them. Var took out his crystal and the Lottl announced, "I am One. We watched as you prepared your little subterfuge and, as we did not understand it, decided to aid you. We heard about the voices to make the others believe there were many of you, so we made many of you appear to be there. We are moving at times just past vision, so they will remain where you told them to stay.

"Von, you will open the portal, so that we may visit our friends and families at home soon?"

"Yes. As soon as we have Vardan Khekth in a position where he can do no further harm. Have you seen him anywhere?"

"We are on only this side of the river so have yet seen no one on the other. There was one who remained on the mountain first in the direction from which these came. He did not enter the fog."

"I see," Var said. "He could see the action of the fog from there, so knows it was not a natural one. I think we won't be able to predict where he will go next."

"He'll find a way to return to Gretlz," Dracht stated, positively. "Any power he has, other than an ability to manipulate a restricted number of things, is there. He does not wish to lose any of that power."

"Then we will have to prevent his getting back there," Von agreed. "Do you think he knows we found his boat?"

Var thought a moment, then nodded. "If we were waiting here we must have.

"Dracht, you come with me and we'll try to find him. He won't move far at night on the mountain and dares not use light.

"I believe I hear Wlad's men coming. I called him on the morn and he can take this bunch to Treglz for shipment home. Von can accompany them and can arrange their transport home. The weapons can join those we took before in the armory at Treglz. We can hope they are never used."

They discussed other plans, then Dracht and Var headed back toward where One said the lone person was on the mountain.

"Var, something is very much not right here," Dracht warned. "Khekth has some kind of plan. He would not sacrifice his few remaining soldiers like this. He would have called them back."

"Yes, I have considered that, my friend," Var replied. "You are right. He has done something I simply can't find a reason for. It is not in his character. Perhaps he has a prepared place to hide near here and intends to wait until he can be certain we are returned to Fendrz and Treglz. He could then make his way to the coast on the river and find passage to Gretlz on a trader.

"That also would seem much out of character." Dracht was deep in thought, but soon shook his head. "If we can find him we'll remember to ask his purpose," he said dryly.

"There he is!" Dracht cried. "He stayed right here! Why?"

"Because that is not Khekth. He left this man here to distract us and cause us to seek him, thus giving him time to escape.

"So! He acted exactly in character after all!"

"But where is he?" Dracht demanded.

Chapter five

"I detect activity moving near the portal," Var warned.

Dracht moved to one side and Var to the other. They waited and a fuzzy outline entered the portal.

"That's one of the Lottl," Dracht said. "You can communicate with it."

Var quickly took the crystal and asked the Lottl if it knew who he was and if Khekth was near.

"We have informed all our people in Lottlland about you and about Kholworld. We have a message system that allows us to inform all of Lottlland in no more than four days of any event.

"The one you refer to as Khekth will arrive in perhaps two flektcs. One referred to as Von has said that three flektcs is equal to two and one quarter hours on Kholworld.

"I am sent to advise you that Khekth will soon arrive."

"How do you send the messages?" Var asked, interested.

"We send messengers from one base to the next and that one sends messengers in the same manner. We are able to move swiftly, as our path is short. An individual, such as Khekth, cannot long sustain a rapid movement as the energy will lessen and the muscle reactions slow. Von wished that we inform you Khekth has among his possessions a large opal set in half silver and half gold and that there is a large ruby ground to a point set in a frame around that. You are to understand what is meant in the relation."

"Ah, yes, my friend, I do," Var said, grimly. "Are there any of your people very near to the entrance to this portal? In a direct line of sight?"

"Line of sight? I do not understand?" the Lottl replied.

"Can you stand at the portal entrance and see a base plant?" Dracht asked.

"Base plant? ... Oh! Yes! The mother. Yes, there is one. I am of it. It is some distance and somewhat higher and can be seen."

"Can you construct a barrier before Khekth arrives here?" Var asked, then explained that piling small rocks between the mother plant and the portal entrance would suffice. The Lottl assured them it could be done, as the angle of view meant a not large wall would be required. Var said it must be done quickly and the Lottl left.

"What was that thing it described?" Dracht asked.

"The opal is a seeker crystal, as you will have guessed, and the ruby collects light that can be directed through the point to burn through even the densest material. This worries me, greatly. That device can do immense damage! We can't stop it!"

"It's light? That's all?" Dracht asked.

"Yes. I have studied much on light and find that heat is often a part of it," Var lectured. "The device takes the heat part and concentrates it to a very fine point, then directs it in a thin line to whatever the thing is pointed at. It will even burn quickly through a diamond, should the ruby be large enough."

"I saw something in that laboratory upstairs as we came down," Dracht said. "I think I can do something about Khekth's little light thrower! I have time! I'll be back in a few minutes!" He raced up the stairs, leaving Var with a startled expression for a moment. Var thought, looked quizzically at the stairs, thought again, sighed, nodded and clicked his tongue for luck. It was just possible the barbarian could defeat the, as he called it, light thrower!

It was getting very close to the time Khekth would appear and Dracht had not returned. Var didn't doubt the time would be very close to what the Lottl predicted.

Var felt a slight stirring that indicated someone was approaching the portal. Khekth was coming and Dracht was not there!

Well, it was entirely possible he could handle it, himself. Surely Khekth wouldn't approach with the light thrower held at the ready and the opal couldn't detect him through the portal.

But the warning from Von was because Khekth *would* probably approach with the device at ready! Where was Dracht?

The form of Khekth materialized in the portal tunnel and he did have the device ready.

Var stepped to the side enough that Khekth couldn't see him and the device would not penetrate the stone frame quickly enough that he couldn't avoid it, but where was Dracht?

Khekth stopped a few meters inside of the tunnel to check the opal and it certainly had detected him if the reaction of Khekth was any indication – but why hadn't he sensed the seeker on him?

Khekth suddenly pointed the ruby directly along the center of the tunnel past Var – to the stairs! There stood Dracht! He had a large bright polished silver bowl in front of him. The red beam hit the bowl and was reflected back to the device in Khekth's hand, which flashed. Khekth dropped it, screamed and fled back along the tunnel.

"What you do with light? You reflect it!" Dracht yelled, triumphantly. "I saw this bowl and have spent my time polishing it to as bright a luster as I could manage! It would seem Khekth doesn't have his light thrower anymore."

"But he is in Nighkt where he can cause great damage," Var pointed out. "My friend, I want you to follow instructions exactly!

"I am going after Khekth. I will neutralize any damaging spells. You are to place that bowl over the copper cube there after I am through the portal. It will make the portal flicker a bit, but will make it safe for you to remove the gold star beside the stream. That will close the portal. You will then move the other six pieces and it will not open again.

"You will then go to Von's portal to await my return there. If Khekth appears at the portal you are to loose a crossbow bolt at him. Shoot him in the head, not the body. He can protect his body, but will be killed if it strikes him in the head – and you are a very good shot."

"Var! Khekth has food and water! There is a good chance he can reach Von's portal! You don't have anything other than your seeker and communication crystals! I know you must do this. I ... wish I could stop you."

"No, my dearest friend. I have the crystals and friends among the Lottl. That is the difference. I will be given food and water. Khekth will be given nothing."

Dracht looked very worried as Var dashed into the portal tunnel. He sighed, swore and did as Var had directed, closing that portal.

He checked over the area carefully, saw the light thrower laying on the dirty stone floor and picked it up. He was fortunate it was pointed to the wall. Khekth's furious face suddenly floated above the opal and the device shot a beam of light into that wall, leaving a smoking hole. The face flickered and disappeared.

Dracht snapped the opal out of the frame and dropped it into his pocket. He carried the frame with him. It was obvious it could be used again should it become necessary to do so – and should he learn *how* to use it!

Var said it collected light, so he would see it wasn't in any light until needed. He headed for the road and the docks. He wanted to be at Von's portal when Var arrived. He didn't much care if they never saw nor heard of Vardan Khekth again.

Var must arrive, unharmed, at that portal!

Var moved quickly into Lottlland and the portal collapsed behind him.

There was no turning back now! There was no one in Gretlz who could open that portal again and Dracht would do as asked and would make it impossible for any accidental re-opening.

How he wished he could have brought the big barbarian with him! He always felt, somehow, safe when Dracht was there, because so much about him was unpredictable. Note the incident where he used a common silver bowl to frustrate a powerful weapon like the light collector! He was able to use whatever was on hand at a given time, while Var must work to a plan.

It was to be a battle of wits with an adversary who was at least as powerful as was he. His first order of business would be to protect the Lottl from such as Vardan Khekth. They had declared themselves his friends and that's what friends did. It wouldn't ever occur to Vardan Herkth that there was any alternative.

There was one other thing he thought of then that he should have thought of before running into that portal!

Khekth could turn a crossbow bolt. He should have warned Dracht to use an iron bolt, as that was much more likely to be effective. Iron had properties that made some spells difficult to use against it. It distorted a focus and one had little time to focus on an object fired at one from a crossbow!

Well, Dracht would cope. He knew about iron and its properties and had the intelligence to connect those details.

There was a seeker spell. He was detected, but that meant only that Khekth would be able to thwart a seeker from him.

He didn't need a seeker. A Lottl was suddenly walking beside him.

"I am to call you Vardan Herkth?" the Lottl asked, as soon as the crystal was produced.

"No. Just Var. How do I address you?"

"Four will suffice. Von has informed that you have a One, Two and Three. It will not become overly complicated until there are many of us, so we are working on a naming system. You might find it difficult to remember whether it is Two Thousand or Two Thousand One with whom you are speaking."

Var wasn't certain if that was humor or merely a statement, but felt it really was meant to be humorous. He smiled at the Lottl. He had always liked people with good strong senses of humor. It generally brought people closer together, as demonstrated with the Gretlz soldiers.

"We will be able to avoid Khekth learning of the Lottl?" Var asked.

"It isn't certain he doesn't know of us. We believe he knows of us, but not that we are ... cognizant. He does not know that we can communicate."

"He is heading for Von's portal?"

"He was in the rocky area to the – what did Von call it? – East? There." He pointed.

"Ah, yes. East. So he feels I will assume he has gone on toward Von's portal and will wait until I have passed.

"I would wonder if he intends to attack me from behind. It would seem his nature to attack from behind."

"We do not understand why anyone would attack anyone else. We will aid you in any way we can. Animals and plants do not consider things in the same manner. We do know that you are possessed of no ill will for us and that Khekth, as you call him, is possessed of ill will for all."

"Yes. You sense such things much in the way a stalker cat knows good from evil – in legend. The fact is they are suspicious of everyone. I think there is a smell of dislike or fear they are more able to detect."

"If I understand what you mean by the term, it is true that you emit different things, they might be what you call odors, that tell us much about you and how you are reacting."

They strolled along, casually chatting about their people until they were well past the rocky area, then Var said he would need a safe place to hide where he could observe Khekth's passing.

"There is room in the mothers," Four pointed out. "You can remain there and we will bring you clean water and some solid sustenance. Von has explained that you must ingest certain things and said to inform you that the taste would probably be strange, but the value as food is safe and high.

"It seems rather inefficient, but it is what is." Var knew that was humor and smiled again. He definitely liked the Lottl.

Four introduced him to Five and he stepped inside the plant that was about twice his height and quite broad. There was ample room and it was actually very comfortable.

He enjoyed a long conversation with Four and Five until Five told him Khekth was passing. He looked to see Khekth pulling a cart along with one hand and with an iron sword in the other hand.

He grinned and talked with his new friends until nightfall. Five became mostly dormant and Four said it must return to its own mother plant. Five would care for it, but such things were considered to be social impositions except in emergencies or when the mother and unit were closely related or when it was a traveler, so would naturally require assistance.

Var understood that travelers were much like the story-tellers of old on Kholworld.

Var left early in the firstdawning. Five had supplied him some rather odd-flavored plants and fresh water for the dawnmeal. He had to admit the food left him satisfied and gave him energy.

Var had gone about six kilometers, following the excellent instructions the Lottl had supplied. He passed several mother plants and always stopped to chat for a few minutes. They told him where Khekth was at a given time and he was staying about two kilometers behind.

There was very little change in the routine, moving across a landscape with little variance of feature for two days, then the first of the more difficult crossings was near. Var decided to stay with Seventeen for the coming night. There would be little reported about Khekth's movements in the area. Luckily, the crossing was only four kilometers and the only other difficult part was twenty or so kilometers beyond that. It was quite close to Von's portal.

One report Var did receive was that Khekth was, apparently, abandoning his cart just before crossing the area, so he was very near the end of his food and supplies.

Var enjoyed an exceptionally pleasant evening with Seventeen. The Lottl were delightful hosts.

In the dawning, after another very nutritious meal and one that proved not so strange in flavor (which was more a matter of Var adapting to the difference, not to a difference in the flavor) Var set off after his quarry. So far, he had seen no evidence that Khekth was doing anything to damage the Lottl. He would remain content to merely follow him at a distance so long as he didn't cause harm.

The trail wasn't particularly difficult for a walker, but he could see it would prove a trial for anyone pulling a cart or carrying a large pack.

He suddenly felt a seeker spell was directed back toward him and countered it. He wondered if Khekth suspected he was followed or if he was simply checking to learn if he was.

Var waited awhile before moving on and was approaching the edge of the badland area when he noted that Khekth was not far ahead, crossing a small ridge. Had he been closer, he would have been detected, so Khekth had waited for some reason.

Var found a small campsite. There was a fire and the bones of a small animal.

So. Khekth was out of food and was finding what he could here. There was little in the normal land, but these badlands did have rodents and a few other animals that were edible. Not knowing what was safe, he wouldn't eat any plants. That would severely limit the time he could remain here, a problem Var wouldn't face, because the Lottl had shown him several more varieties of plants that he could safely eat.

Var approached the little ridge carefully. Just beyond should be the regular and much flatter landscape. He would be as visible crossing the ridge as Khekth had been if from the opposite direction.

Var studied the lay of the land and found there was some protection in a copse of small bushy trees in one spot. It was a matter of half a kilometer detour, which would be worth the extra time and energy.

He could then see Khekth on the horizon. He wouldn't be so visible to Khekth with the ridge behind him, but would move with caution.

A day and a half and they would be at Von's portal. Var wasn't so sure he would be glad the trip was finished because he was making a lot of new friends among the Lottl as he traveled.

He definitely thought names for the people would be needed, though.

Little of any import transpired the following day. Var took more time to speak with the Lottl as he moved, because Khekth was moving much more slowly and carefully now, clearly expecting someone would be waiting for him at the portal and possibly would be a certain distance inside in Lottlland. He perhaps expected an ambush.

He stopped just before the second badlands area late in the afternoon and made a small camp. The Lottl were watching and reporting on his every move. They could approach quite closely here because there were fogs in the area, due to the small clean stream that ran through, creating the badlands.

Var was amused that what would be the good lands on Kholworld were the badlands to the Lottl. A stream with this lush growth and the attendant life was deadly to the Lottl because their roots would stay moist and fungi would soon infect and kill them.

The units could tolerate the higher moisture because they could move back out of it and absorbed some moisture from the fogs, plus the fact the fog was where they were best adapted to hide.

Var could see the small fire Khekth made about a quarter of a kilometer ahead, so stayed with (actually inside the many protective branches of) Twenty Nine. He had learned a few of the things the Lottl found humorous and was able to joke with them a bit and found he was well-adjusted to the food offered, finding it actually tasty.

From this point forward would be the more difficult part of his journey. Khekth would be excessively wary. He might tend to set traps. He often used the seeker and was puzzled that there was no one detected. He would have the natural feeling denizens of Kholworld experienced of being constantly watched while in Nighkt.

Well, he was!

In the morning Var moved carefully, with the aid of the Lottl, into a plant very close to Khekth, who seemed to be searching for something.

"Did he come through here when he went toward Gretlz?" Var asked the Lottl.

"No, he was perhaps half a kilometer west of here."

"He has made a plan. He left something. I will want to go to where he came out of the badlands. I must find what he left!"

He was taken back and around to a spot where there were two distinctive rocks. They had seams of quartzite that sparkled in the sunlight. That was where Khekth came onto the plain.

Var bid the Lottl good fortune and moved slowly along the path into the area. There were very small signs that someone had been through.

Var finally found a little cave where there was a chest held in a sealer spell. If he broke that spell Khekth would know it.

Why didn't Khekth detect the spell and come directly here? It was, after all, *his* spell! Something was very wrong! Var studied the chest and sighed inwardly. It had been opened, recently, within an hour or so. Khekth had come here to retrieve something.

And to set a trap. If that chest were opened, Var would not live long. It was possible Khekth saw him come into the cave.

No. He was *not* where he could see the cave when Var entered. With the lush vegetation surrounding the spot he would have to be very close and the natural talents of Var would have warned him. He was probably finding a high point to set up his seeker.

Var chanced a small seeker search, a very quick one. Khekth was a few hundred meters south and above. He had detected Var's seeker. It was too fast for him to know the direction it came from, but he was suddenly moving toward this cave – and there was no way out!

Var peered into the darkness behind and sent a small flash of light along the tunnel. It seemed quite deep, so he moved into the darkness. With only a little luck he could avoid detection and Khekth would not stay long there.

Var could well understand that Khekth would be cautious and not in a very great hurry to approach Von's portal. He would know for a certainty that there would be someone watching. His logical strategy would be to remain here until Von placed someone to watch the portal who had no powers and he could exit inside a hider spell. He couldn't know that was not going to happen.

Var went around three bends into a little side cave to wait until Khekth again left the cave. He was fairly sure he would, because there was no particular reason anyone would stay there. It had little to offer except as a possible refuge in the night.

Khekth was again using a seeker. Why? Inside the cave? Had something alerted him to Var's presence?

Var tried to picture the cave, the trail leading to it and everywhere he'd been. The trail was hard rock that would show nothing, as was the floor of the cave. There shouldn't be anything. There was no contact spell or such. They were easy to detect and avoid.

Something not a spell.

Var almost exclaimed aloud. He had so hard concentrated on spells that he might well have tripped some simple mechanical trap. A piece of fine thread or vine, stacked pebbles, a seemingly innocent tiny bit of dust. There were thousands of ways to place a trap.

There were small animals, rodents mostly, in the area. Khekth could not be absolutely certain that any such trap wasn't disturbed by such as those.

Khekth was setting up a very powerful seeker, so he wasn't taking care to not be discovered anymore, which meant he knew full well that someone was there who knew he was there. Var was not in a good position and wished he'd had the simple common sense to bring along a crossbow. He knew he could depend on help from the Lottl and had thus foregone carrying any such weapon.

The Lottl could not help him here, had they even know he might need such aid. They didn't often come into what they considered dangerous badlands. It would be to Vardan Herkth to help Vardan Herkth.

What were the options open to him?

He didn't fear Khekth, so far as the spells and such went, because he had equal or superior powers, in those areas, but Khekth might well have more simple resources, such as the crossbow Var wished he had.

All he had was surprise. Perhaps he could use that to advantage. He had to act quickly or the seeker would take that advantage away.

He moved back along the cave to find Khekth sitting on a boulder, working with the seeker. He came silently behind Khekth and announced, "You won't need that. It didn't find me before so it won't be much help now.

"I trust you have enjoyed your journey across Nighkt. It is a fascinating place, if a bit lacking in variety in the landscape.

"Did you really have the arrogance to believe you could simply move into Fendrz and Treglz in such an obvious manner?

"Ah, well! It's going to be interesting to see how you manage to return to Kholworld! You are not a popular person there!"

Khekth stared a moment in shocked silence, then picked up a light collector to point at Var. "You are going to ensure that my return is a safe one!"

"Really?" Var replied. "You point that silly useless thing at me here in a dark cave? Didn't my companion, a simple barbarian with only the most limited of powers, demonstrate that such devices are somewhat prone to failure?"

Khekth nodded and placed the device on the rock and moved toward the chest. Var moved to sit on the flat rock beside the light thrower, pick it up, turn it over, and say it seemed very well-constructed. It was a fortunate thing for him there was no light to power it here.

He sighed and put it back down and moved back toward the chest. Khekth circled back close to the rock.

"Well, shall we go back to Kholworld and end this game of hider-seeker?" Var asked.

Khekth stared a long moment more, moved close to the boulder, raised his arms above his head and spun, disappearing before Var's eyes.

That spell would be effective for only a few seconds, but Khekth was out of the cave and gone. He had taken the light thrower with him, but left the chest. Var opened it to see seeker crystals and a few devices. There was a large carved ivory box with a clear crystal lid. It was empty. Khekth had a power crystal and that could be very bad for anyone he met. It could be bad for the Lottl.

Var took the chest and went quickly to the Lottl nearby to warn them to not let Khekth know of their existence. The warning would be spread.

Now Var had the task of finding Khekth and his light thrower – and that power crystal.

The Lottl would deliver the chest to Von and Dracht and would explain what Var planned to do. That power crystal was a dangerous thing in the hands of such as Khekth. It could be used a number of ways to thwart anything Var might have done to control and locate Khekth.

If Khekth suspected he had done anything.

Chapter six

Dracht made his way to Von and the portal. He carefully explained all that Var had done, that he was in Nighkt and that Khekth must come to the portal to survive. He could live in Nighkt for only a limited time. He showed Von the light thrower and Von promised to read about its use and to help him learn to use it if it didn't require the sorcerers' mind power. The seeker opal did, but the light thrower might well not and one didn't need a seeker crystal when he was already directly looking at his target! There would be a wait of at least four days, probably more, and Dracht didn't for a single second believe Var would have an easy time of it, except that his nature would make him spend time learning about the Lottl and befriending them.

He went to Treglz to spend some time with Fekth, who tried to explain how the ruby could store light for a time and releases it at once. It was a matter of making the light reflect back and forth inside the ruby until a place was opened for it to exit. The ruby didn't get hot because the light had to be absorbed to produce heat and it was merely reflecting inside while stored. It didn't make any sense to Dracht, but Fekth was brilliant in understanding such strange abstract concepts. It did leave Dracht feeling he could use the light thrower.

He next checked his crossbow carefully and thought (as Var predicted) about the fact that a sorcerer worth the name could turn a crossbow bolt enough to make it miss and that iron made a spell work very slowly or not at all, so he soon fashioned a good iron shaft.

He then went back to the portal. Von was staying there to greet the Lottl as they passed back and forth. Von would go into Nighkt and stay the night at times, saying the Lottl were excellent hosts and provided comfortable quarters for him while he was there. He stayed the night of the third day after Dracht returned and reported that Khekth was in what the Lottl called the badlands, only a few kilometers away, and that Var was also going into the area.

Dracht took the light thrower to a nearby safe spot and tried various ways to make it work. He was becoming frustrated with it when Von came to say that the light was released, according to his book, when a small pin was dropped from in front of the point.

There was, indeed, a small pin there. Dracht studied it carefully and saw that there was a trip lever directly behind the ruby where his thumb would rest very easily.

He pointed the crystal at a large boulder and depressed the lever. A bright glowing red line flashed. That was all.

The line *did* strike the boulder, so he went close to inspect and found a very hot spot with a very small hole in the center. He pushed a straw into the hole and it went deeper than the third of a meter length of the straw.

That would certainly be enough to go through a person!

Aim for the head, because he can protect his body. If the crossbow failed, perhaps the light thrower wouldn't. All he had to do was leave it in the direct sunlight for a few minutes. Fekth had explained that all the light that struck the crystal in the time it was there would be stored for later use, though there was some leakage, meaning it must be used within perhaps ten minutes to be most effective.

Dracht argued that he could stand in direct sunlight for hours and wouldn't be burned much if at all.

"But if you took all the heat that struck your entire body in an hour and released it all at once on a spot the size of a spicegreen seed it would certainly burn that spot com-pletely through your body," Fekth pointed out. "That is, in effect, what the light thrower does.

"You have used a lens to start a fire, I'm sure. All that does is focus most of the light striking the lens to a small point and you see how quickly the tight concentration of light will start a fire. Imagine that effect made a thousand times stronger on a point one tenth as large!"

Now *that*, he understood!

Whatever, he would be as ready as possible for Vardan Khekth and would have both a plan and an alternative plan.

Fekth said he saw no reason there would be a limit on how many times the crystal could be, as he called it, "Charged, discharged, recharged and redischarged." Dracht spent some time learning to focus the point on a small spot and could hit within the area of a halfcredit coin at ten meters almost every time.

He then practiced until he attained the same accuracy with the crossbow.

Dracht was going to be ready for anything – he hoped.


"Something is not right here," Von complained. "They should have arrived, but I would think Khekth will wait until he feels we will become a bit negligent in our guard.

"What worries me is that Vardan Herkth has not come."

"The Lottl said he was in good spirits and health," Dracht replied. "I worry that he'll think he can handle Khekth alone and in Nighkt. He isn't invulnerable.

"Von, let's go to Nighkt and speak with the Lottl. They may not have understood something that will be clear to us."

Von nodded and they went to the portal. Two Lottl were just then coming through, carrying a large carved chest. Von brought out the communicator crystal and the Lottl explained that Var had asked them to deliver the chest and to tell them that it had belonged to Khekth. Von would know the implications of the items inside.

Dracht was eager to open the chest, but Von spoke with the Lottl for a few minutes, then had them bring it outside the area of the portal. He said it was possible Khekth could reach influence to anything very close.

They opened the chest and Von staggered. "What is it?!" Dracht demanded.

"The ivory chest! It is empty! Khekth has a power crystal! He has it in direct contact!"

"Which means?"

"That he can do truly horrific damage and can effectively hide from even Herkth!"

Dracht thought grim thoughts for a moment, then said Khekth had a habit of overlooking details and his friend would use that fact against him. Var would also know the dangers to himself and others from that power crystal and would do something to neutralize it.

"Well, I can see that Khekth might tend to underestimate Herkth," Von agreed.

"And I think Var hopes Khekth will greatly overestimate him," Dracht replied, grinning. "You will find that Khekth has no monopoly on being sneaky!"

"Overestimate him?" Von asked, confused.

"It is our baseless fears that do us in. If there is good reason for the fear it protects us. If we fear things that are no danger, we make that danger for ourselves. When a person tries to avoid walking on one side of a street he must travel, he walks on the other. Too often, the other side is where the actual danger lies."

"I worry," Von said, chancing a small grin of his own.

"Worry?"

"That almost made sense."

"Yeah, I know. Var usually almost makes sense. It's his most charming and maddening trait."

"It was very clear to me," a Lottl said. "Var has done something to make Khekth walk the far side of this street thing, which I will assume is a path, and the danger is there to him, not on the side where Var walks.

"There is a moral story among my people of a screehawk captured by a baahkbear, which is a large animal that has some strange innate hatred of screehawks, possibly of their overly raucous noisiness.

"The screehawk is known as a clever bird and the baahkbear is a rather stupid animal.

"The baahkbear was trying to decide what to do to torture and kill the screehawk. It wished to incite as much fear and pain as possible.

"The screehawk said it was captured and must accept its fate. It was helpless as to what the baahkbear did with it and it had no hope of mercy, but still wished to ask one small one.

"Please do *not* throw it off the cliff! Do anything it wanted, but please do *not* throw it off the cliff.

"Of course, the baahkbear, falling from the cliff, would be mangled and torn when it struck the rocks below – which was a horrible death.

"The baahkbear, predictably for such a stupid being, threw the screehawk off the cliff. The screehawk flew away calling back its thanks for that small mercy."

"Another likeness in our people," Dracht said. "We have such a story about a plopjumper and a stalkercat. It begged the stupid stalkercat *not* to throw it into that rushing river!"

"Ah, of course! And the plopjumper is a water animal as the screehawk is a flying animal?" the Lottl asked.

"Yes. It is what we refer to as an amphibian, which is an animal that lives part of the time in the water and part on land, as the screehawk is an animal that lives part of the time in the air and part of the time on the land.

"There is a small crystal missing from the case. A locator crystal. It is very small and nothing can be read from it except direction."

"Won't Khekth detect it?" Dracht asked.

"Only if he deliberately seeks that crystal and he will probably not, as it is his crystal. If he used it, it will possibly be here on Kholworld and can't be used from Nighkt. I suspect it was one he used when he placed the chest wherever Herkth found it to be able to find it easily. He will have placed it where a crystal is expected to be seen, so it will not be noted."

"But Var would note it?" a Lottl asked.

"Yes, certainly," Von answered.

"So Var has found the crystal and it is with Khekth and he can know generally where Khekth is by locating it!" Dracht cried. "That means he has made a plan. It is something to do with things Khekth has put on Nighkt!"

"Whatever it is will be found in the badlands," a Lottl suggested. "Were it in any other place we would know of it."

"Damnation!" Dracht exclaimed. "Now I don't know if he wants me to come to him!"

"No. He would have sent any such request with us," a Lottl pointed out.

"Logical!" Von agreed. "The crystal is not good for determining distance, only direction, so is limited in use, I fear."

"No! Fekth has told me of angles!" Dracht argued. "If one knows where a thing is from two places, even very close together places, and he knows how far apart those two places are he can know to within meters of where an object is!"

"Ah, yes. It will be the spot where the two angles intersect," a Lottl agreed. "A distance and the angle can be figured from another distance *between* the two angles. We call it triangle formulation.

"Another likeness in our people! We both are fascinated by what we Lottl call mathematical concepts and formulations. It is a way to make numbers explain nature.

"I believe our people, as different as they may be, are more alike!"

"Except in one area, I agree," Dracht said. "I think you do not have people like Khekth."

"Ah, yes. There is that," the Lottl replied.


Another day and no word from Var. Von was studying the light thrower, looked thoughtful, removed two crystals from his case, placed them carefully, one to either side of the device, and concentrated. A very insubstantial shadow was seen in what appeared to be a large tree above a wispy stream.

"This is Khekth's crystal and can locate him within certain small restrictions," Von explained. "I think he cannot detect its use from Kholworld. I have learned only that he is hiding in a tree within twenty four kilometers of this portal. I imagine it will be half of that, because it is a seeking from here.

"He is holding something. I believe it is a light thrower. I wonder if Vardan Herkth knows he has that one."

"I'd think that he would," Dracht replied and pointed to the one between the crystals. Von looked quizzically at it, then at the thrower, looked puzzled, then suddenly exclaimed, "Of course! It has small crystals in the frame and Var has seen that the locator is one of them!"

"Which means he can protect himself from it," Dracht agreed. "I wonder if Var has a plan or if he'll just take things as they happen. I don't understand why he hasn't acted before now."

"He strongly suspects Khekth has something else hidden there and is determined to find it."

"That would fit. I am going to Nighkt to visit with the Lottl. I can use the communication crystal Khekth left in his chest can't I?"

"No, but we can spend some time finding a way that can be done. It will be needed, as our people intermingle more. We can't have a vardan or vondar present at all times for all of them.

"The crystal works because it has the ability to open a trained mind to another mind. That's as close as I can explain it.

"Now the Lottl can use it when we activate it because it's not greatly unlike the way they communicate among themselves. The words we hear are not spoken, they appear in our ears – or our minds, more accurately.

"If the talent to use the crystal is already in one half of the users it is only necessary to find something in your mind to open yourself to it – and that happens when you speak with the Lottl when I'm present, because I am not acting as an intermediary.

"Very well. It is something I do that I'm not aware I'm doing, so let us both go to Nighkt. So long as Khekth is in the badlands he is no closer than two kilometers to the portal and I can carry the light thrower with a spell on it to inform me if he comes within those two kilometers and we can return before he can arrive here.

"I am going to teach you how to use a communicator crystal."

"Will I be able to use others if I can use the communicator?"

"I think probably not. The communicator doesn't require the mind force to any extent. Others require quite a lot. My own theory is that a vardan is one who possesses a greater talent in that area. Even a vardan such as Fekth doesn't possess the talent to a very great degree, as he is first to confess. He can use the communicator crystal without extra thought or concentration so it seems reasonable to believe these crystals require little of the talent."

"One small thing before we go. If Khekth had a locator crystal in the frame of that light thrower he will have one in this one."

Von looked a bit startled, nodded and very carefully studied the light thrower. He found a small crystal, a not very significant one for value or rarity, and pried it out of the frame with his knife, then searched around the cave a moment until he found a pebble of like size with red and black striations, inserted it into the socket and bent the prongs to hold it in place.

"Shall we go? I will leave this crystal in Khekth's chest. If he can use it he will believe the light thrower is here."

They went through the portal and to Four, where they spent a little more than an hour, but Dracht learned to use the crystal. Once the Lottl was focused on it the communicator could be used with ease. Four was, in Dracht's mind, a lot of fun. It had a wonderful sense of humor that came from an unexpected angle that Von often didn't see, it becoming a joke between Four and Dracht. Dracht noted the jokes were not hurtful in any way, but were simple fun.

While they were there  two of the units brought in a third, who seemed to be broken apart. They placed it into the mother plant and the head and part of the upper chest area were removed and the lower parts carried out. Four explained that the body would grow back in perhaps forty days with the help of the mother. The brain part was unharmed. Had it been damaged, the life force would have been extracted and saved and the entire "carcass" carried out. Von nor Dracht understood the process, but both were aware that the Lottl were plants, so they probably couldn't understand it in a real sense.

Four explained that the "life force" was the complete memory of the unit. That was never lost. Four had memory stretching back many hundreds of years. It was an individual by its own memories that began when it was first separated from its mother, ninety two years ago.

If a "new" Lottl grew from a seed, as would happen on Kholworld to a very limited extent, it would have many memories from several established mothers "donated" to it and would become a mother after about twenty years, starting another "family".

They discussed the fact that the people of Kholworld had no memories and that the only memories "saved" were written down in books.

"It seems so much would be lost," Four said.

"But we do not have millions of memories of trivial or useless things kept for generation after generation," Von pointed out.

"Nor do we. We can remove the great majority of such things, and do. We have to be careful, in that what is of importance today can become meaningless tomorrow while what is useless today might as easily become vastly important tomorrow."

After the philosophical discussions Dracht and Von returned to the portal and Kholworld to await further developments. Von had set a spell to warn him if Khekth approached the portal or if Var called and they slept. It had been a long time since they could relax so well, knowing that Var was probably in no extreme danger.

Still, they both wondered why Var was being so cautious about Khekth. What was there other than Khekth's power crystal to make such a step necessary?

The following day was much like the others. Dracht went into Nighkt to speak with the Lottl, who enjoyed speaking of the differences in the barbarian societies, which Dracht knew little of, and the more "civilized" societies of the towns. Dracht was amazed at how much was shared among the Lottl and they were amazed that so little was shared among Dracht's people. They didn't understand the drive in animals toward competition for material things. They showed Dracht where many beautiful crystals were found in a strange whitish clay vein. They would sometimes take a particularly fine stone to the mother plant because they had a strong sense of beauty. These were opals and emeralds!

Dracht caught himself as he was gathering some of the stones. He compared those he had and tossed all but one of each type back. These were the property of the Lottl, even if they didn't even understand what property was and he would respect that. They had told him he could have all the crystals he wanted and he would keep these few as remembrances, not treasures – though such meaningful remembrances were the finest of all treasures, to his way of thinking.

He was greatly influenced by the Lottl. He knew it then. A very short time ago he would have gathered every stone he could find. He would then be vastly wealthy when he returned with them to Kholworld.

He returned to the portal to find Von had been fishing and was cooking a delicious meal of fish, spicegreens and baked whitebeans. They enjoyed the food, then sat around discussing the Lottl and the way societies on Kholworld were going to be changed because of them. The consensus was that little would change except in the near areas to the lands the Lottl would use to establish colonies.

It was a very clear warm night and the cookfire made dancing shadows on the nearby bushes and rocks. Two and Three came to sit, talking, and soon One joined them. Dracht showed them the stones and told of how Four showed them to him. They said there were many areas where such stones could be easily found. The Lottl had known of them since the time of the old fire mountains.

That led to a discussion of the time many thousands of years past when Lottlland had several volcanoes. There were none on the nearer lands now, but there were some far to the west and north and another group at the extreme south where the ice never melted.

The Lottl were preparing to return to their mother plants when Var stepped from the portal.

Chapter seven

Var carefully scanned the area and looked at his seeker, where a dot was shown in light on one side. He had found the locator on the frame to the light thrower and had touched it to sense how to find it, then had deliberately laid the thing back on the rock for Khekth to take. Khekth was in the direction of the light spot. Var could easily determine very nearly where he was by the time and change in direction.

Var would have to find where Khekth had hidden that power crystal. Had he taken it while in the cave he would have used it against anyone who challenged him – and Var had challenged him, very certainly.

Khekth had definitely been in Nighkt many times. He was too sure of himself and of the place to have not been, though Var doubted very much he had been in this area. He had been near Gretlz and may have hidden things there. That would very certainly not include a power crystal. Khekth wouldn't have more than the one. No vardan had more than one.  If Var could get that crystal he could reasonably forget about Khekth, because he would be far too limited to do much damage in Lottlland *or* Kholworld.

The rest of Khekth's devices would go with the chest to Von, who could study them and learn what else might be used, later. The light thrower and power crystal were all that really mattered here and now and the use of either would depend on Khekth being able to find Var and to face him. So long as the locator would keep Var informed of the general whereabouts of Khekth, that facing could be avoided.

Var's most difficult problem would be to find a way to get his hands on the crystal. That would not happen so long as Khekth held it. He would have to contrive to force Khekth to try to hide it somewhere.

That would be a matter of when Khekth must seek food. He could not carry the crystal when he sought food because animals could sense it and would stay far away from it. Khekth would not know which plants might be safe to consume, so must seek animal food.

He could carry the crystal, should he find a way to catch fish. It did not repel them. There was a cool stream through the center of the badlands.

Var went to the stream to see it was a clear clean flow. It was fairly deep at this spot and the velocity of the flow told him it was generally that deep or the water would flow slower in those parts that were deepest. That would mean fish would be difficult to catch unless there were side tributaries that were not so swift or so deep.

Khekth was moving, but very slowly. It didn't seem reasonable that he would move that slowly, so he was either approaching or moving away along the stream, so lateral movement would be minimal.

Var moved away from the stream, but stayed close enough to see it. Khekth would check the seeker crystal on the light thrower from time to time, but Var could easily avoid detection by that.

So. Khekth had no other seeker. That could prove most important.

It was more than three hours later before Var knew Khekth was moving away from him. Considering the time factor he was certainly at the limit of where he could have gone at any time before to hide anything, so what was he doing?

It would soon be getting dark, so Var found a comfortable spot in a protected cleft in the rock face where he could see the river. He built a small fire, then took off his clothes and went into the cool stream to bathe, then returned to the fire with the clothes he had washed in the stream and hung them to dry near the fire.

He checked his pockets to be sure there was nothing he had forgotten and found a tiny strange bright crystal. It was a blue beryl, very rare and possessing powers.

So. When had Khekth gotten close enough to place that crystal?

In the cave. After the disappearing spell. He was close to the rock where the light thrower was left. Therefore, Khekth knew he was there and generally where he was, the same as he knew from the crystal on the light thrower where Khekth was.

He knew about this crystal, Khekth did *not* know he could follow him with the crystal on the light thrower.

He grinned and took the crystal to the stream, placed it on a dried piece of wood and pushed it into the stream, then quickly retrieved it. He would not travel at night here and Khekth would know that. He would send it on its way in the morning.

He checked to see that Khekth was moving. At night?

On the stream. He either had a raft or had decided to send that locator crystal on the same kind of voyage Var was planning to send the crystal he'd found. At the rate the stream was moving, it would pass in perhaps three hours.

Var thought for a few minutes, then took the crystal to the hill not far away and called to the Lottl with the caller. It was not long before one came. He asked that it carry the crystal out of the badlands and close to the portal. He explained what he was doing. Which amused the Lottl, who said it wasn't necessary to explain. It was more than happy to assist.

They spoke for a few minutes, then Var went back to his camp. The crystal passed on schedule and it was only a small bowl, from what Var could see in the darkness.

Well, he wouldn't know where Khekth was now, but Khekth wouldn't know where he was, either. Regardless, Khekth couldn't be there in less than nine hours, so Var slept.

In the morning Var spent some time trying to decide what Khekth might do and decided he had made a small mistake in sending the locator crystal to the portal because Khekth would not go there.

*Until he had his power crystal!*

Time for some logical thinking. Khekth may have suspected the crystal on the light thrower, but couldn't be sure. There was no sign there that is was in use, but there was a way to determine if it was and that was with the power crystal.

Khekth had gone a great distance and had discovered the crystal was being used, so the crystal had been what he was seeking, as Var had suspected.

Khekth now had the power crystal.

He would go to the portal. He was surely going to be in need of food soon. He may have been able to capture animals as he went after the crystal, but couldn't while he had the crystal on his person.

He believed Var was already at or near the portal, so would be less wary in that belief.

He would believe it safe to move onto the dry plain area to return to the portal, not knowing of the Lottl.

*No*! Possibly knowing *of* them, but not knowing that the Lottl could communicate! He would not know they were highly intelligent beings and certainly not that the plants he was passing were the Lottl.

Var took the time for an intense inspection, both visually and with spells, of everything he had with him. He wanted nothing on his person that Khekth could detect with that power crystal.

He carefully cleaned the area where he'd had the fire and headed toward the portal. He had to find a way to counter that power crystal or to get it. There was no other way. If he had his own power crystal he could chance a fight, but would have no chance of survival if he were to face Khekth with that crystal in his possession.

Khekth would have the crystal and the light thrower, but could probably not use them at the same time.

Var went to the Lottl they called Two near the portal and had a long discussion. He held nothing back. Two sent messengers to ask One and Three to send units and Var repeated what seemed to be the problem.

The Lottl would help any way they could, but Var didn't want them exposed to the dangers of the things Khekth might use.

"Friend Var," One chided. "You do not well understand us. We are not in any real danger from such as Khekth. Units, such as myself, can be totally destroyed and it will affect very little. If we are merely damaged we can be regrown.

"We understand that Khekth is capable of damaging the mother, but he does not know of the mothers. He has seen some few units from a distance and is not sure of our nature.

"You have indicated that his attention must remain on only one object, thus we can supply confusion that will give you opportunities to defeat him."

"But we consider the units as individuals," Var pointed out. "We do not wish to cause you pain."

"We do not know pain," Three said. "We are aware of damage and we are *not* individuals. We are parts. The mother is the individual.

"Friend Var, we will protect the mother first in all things. That is our basic function and our nature. We will also protect our friends. If every unit from a mother is destroyed she will be somewhat sad, but will grow as many more as are needed. We are then given the memories and talents needed for our purpose and everything will be back to normal in only a few days.

"You speak to all of us and to the mother when you speak to any of us. All information is given to the mother each time we return. All that can be lost is what happens after we leave and before we return.

"We will do everything we can to help you and can do it at a distance from the mother. Khekth will not know of the mother, so all things are very safe, in reality."

"Then I believe we can work together to rid this world and Kholworld of such as Khekth. If we can divert his attention from the power crystal, and it is a very difficult thing to control, we can use something else to defeat him. The crystal can protect him from anything on a straight line through his position to what is in front of him. Anyone at even a very slight angle behind him is not in its area of influence.

"I wish we had some of the things in my study to use here, but I did not bring weapons.

"We will make do."

"Friend Dracht has what he refers to as a light thrower," Two said. "He has learned to use it very well, I believe, and he has what he calls a crossbow iron bolt or something that he is able to accurately use to strike a very small object at perhaps twenty meters distance."

"Yes!" Var cried. "I should have known Dracht would think to pick up the light thrower in Gretlz! He is a very astute observer.

"He can use it? He has learned?"

"Vardan Fekth and Von came with him and they showed him how it operates," Three said. "I remember they said he cannot use the seeker because that takes the sorcerer's talent, but he can use the device because it is what Fekth calls mechanical."

"Then I am much more comfortable with the gamble we must take. This is not a decided battle. That could only be if we could be sure what Khekth will do, and we can't. He is not rational in his methods or decisions."

"And you are?" Two asked, innocently, but Var could sense the humor.

"I make a personal choice to face a more powerful foe in a life or death encounter, a foe who is both insane and unpredictable, and you wonder at my sanity? Why?" Var asked, as innocently.

They made small jokes, then Var went to the portal and through.

"Var! We thought you'd found a pleasant spot in Nighkt and decided to settle there!" Dracht greeted, embracing the sorcerer. "I'd hoped you were going to report that Khekth is no more, but you don't look like that's the case."

"Khekth is coming to the portal, I believe, and he has his power crystal with him," Var replied. Von groaned.

"I suppose that means we're going to have a battle," Dracht said. "I've learned a few things that can be useful."

"So I've been told," Var said. "The Lottl can help tremendously and we can be prepared to handle the situation from several angles — and I mean that both literally and figuratively.

"We will have to call on all the arts we know as well as brute force and trickery."

"You have a general plan?" Von asked. "Do you think it wise to involve the Lottl?"

"They have explained some things to me that I had never before considered. It is their choice and they are in little real danger."

"Oh? Really?" Dracht asked. "Then they won't be harmed by a light thrower or that power crystal?"

"No. They've explained about that. They're *plants*, Dracht! If Khekth burns a hole through them it will grow back with little damage. If he cuts them into pieces the mother can restore them to perfect health in a few days. They don't feel pain, though they know when there is damage. What they know of pain is only what was explained to them.

"Von, the only important thing to them is that the mother is not in danger and there is no mother close to the portal enough that it would be in danger. We have already shielded the one with direct sight with a wall of stones. The units and I did that.

"We will just have to do something to divide Khekth's attention for only a short moment, then Dracht can use the light thrower or the iron bolt on the crossbow.

"Aim for the head, Dracht. That is important.

"We will place ourselves where I will be directly in front of him and the two of you will be behind, as I'm sure Von has instructed. The power crystal is a mighty weapon for what is in *front* of the holder, but is of little use as to what's *behind.* That will divide his attention three ways and he won't be able to direct the power crystal totally to me without then losing concentration on one or both of you."

"But that is not enough to stop him, because it only evens out the power between the two of you and we can't act unless there is more of a ... I see! That is where the Lottl become part of the plan!"

"Yes. Lottl will approach from all angles," Var agreed. "He will be able to protect himself to an extent, but not to attack."

"You have to add some confusion, or rather, uncertainty," Von pointed out. "He can protect himself very well only so long as he can know with any certainty where everyone is in relation to his position at the time."

"I will have the Lottl move around and he will tend to lose focus."

"What? You're both stupid?" Dracht asked, shaking his head. "That's the easiest part!"

"It is?"

"Are you, or are you not, known as the Lord of Fogs?"

Both Var and Von looked a bit shocked, then embarrassed. They started to giggle.

"Gheesh! If you didn't have someone around to point out the obvious you'd get yourselves and half of Lottlland *and* Kholworld killed!" Dracht accused. They all started joking then. Several of the Lottl came, they explained and were joined in the joking.

But this was a deadly serious undertaking and they all knew it.

"This waiting is going to be the hardest thing to withstand," Dracht complained. "We are going to be tired and he'll use that against us. I think he plans to deliberately keep us from getting any rest. He knows we're waiting and watching."

"I don't know about you, but I intend to get plenty of sleep and rest and a good meal as well," Var said. "I will, of course, place this call crystal beside my head."

"I can be as stupid as you, it seems! The Lottl will tell us when he comes." They were in fair spirits as they ate the tasty meal and prepared for the night. Var wondered if Khekth was getting any sleep, then reasoned he would definitely not appear until he was well-rested.

But he didn't have food.

Maybe he was able to save something.

He would depend on Khekth being in the very best condition as to rest and sustenance, as a matter of course. Better to take a precaution and not need it than to need one not taken! They slept well and were refreshed with the dawn. The Lottl reported that they had not seen any sign of

Khekth, whatever. He had not moved onto the plains so was still somewhere in the badlands.

That didn't make any sense. He wouldn't stay in the badlands to travel when he thought Var had come to the portal!

"Von ... something is very wrong here!" Var insisted. "We have to know where he is and what he plans! He simply cannot hope to survive there for long!"

"Var, that crystal the Lottl brought," Dracht asked. "Is it connected to Khekth somehow?"

Var thought, then said it wouldn't be of any use to him if it wasn't, but there was nothing it could tell them they didn't already know.

"Could it tell you if he's alive?" Dracht asked. "What if he stepped in a strikerserpent nest? Could he save himself with what he has there? If he fell off of a cliff?"

Var thought again and agreed it could tell them that. If Khekth was dead the crystal would have no point of focus.

Von got the beryl and they sat at the entrance to the portal to concentrate with a seeker crystal to either side of it. A small spot of light shown for a few seconds, then faded, then was back, then faded.

"What does that mean?" Dracht asked.

"I don't *know!*" Var cried. "It indicates both that he is alive and dead!"

They thought for a few minutes longer, then tried again with the same result. Dracht asked Var exactly which direction Khekth was from their position. Var pointed south and west.

"How far?" Dracht asked.

"Perhaps two hundred thirty kilometers," Var answered.

"Which would be about twenty kilometers into the straits between Fendrz and Gretlz? Would that be awfully close to Waderbird Island?"

Var sighed and took the crystal to Kholworld and set it up with the seekers. There was a very strong light floating just above it.

"He had a portal on the island!" Von cried. "He's already back in Gretlz!"

"No, but he's on Waderbird Island," Dracht argued. "He'll stay there for awhile to regroup his forces. He'll have to recruit new soldiers because those we took home will not stand against us.

"Now what?"

"Now we go to Fendrz and collect a few things, then we go calling on Vardan Khekth," Var snarled. "I can be very damned sure he won't detect me here and he won't dare to use a seeker that I can detect."

"Var, let's go to where his portal is here," Dracht said, thinking. "There's something you're not considering, I think. Something that's very important."

"What is that, my friend?"

"There is no way that Khekth left a portal open on Waderbird Island."

"And there is that stream in the badlands that will keep it open safely. It would be wise to close it.

"Dracht, this means he knows how to open a portal from the end opposite the one we know, where we don't even know how! He is a very intelligent person, perhaps a genius."

"Perhaps. He's also insane."

"It will take us about four days to get there on the plains in Lottlland. We can't carry much, but I must take a few things.

"Dracht, we'll go through his portal. I'll have the Lottl dismantle it when we're through.

"I wish we could take a mountbeast or two! It would save us three days and we could carry the things we'll need!"

"Perhaps you can," Von suggested. "If you travel close to the badlands, there is forage for them there. They will know if they can eat it because animals know those things, somehow.

"We have mountbeast here that we came on.

"I can go to Waderbird Island. Khekth does not know me, has never seen me. I can gather the things you will need from here and meet you there with them."

"Better to meet us at Southpoint Harbor," Dracht suggested. "It's four kilometers away and there are boats all the time. If you take that power stuff to Waderbird he'll know. He might not pay too much attention to Southpoint because it's only a small fishing village and some docks."

They agreed to that. They called their favorite mountbeasts, loaded a few supplies and went through the portal, though the mountbeasts made it *quite* plain they didn't appreciate being taken through.

Var and Dracht spoke with the Lottl awhile, then set off to find the portal. Var had an idea of where it was located, so was able to take them close, then the sorcerer's talent took them to the portal. It was quite small and they would barely fit through. Dracht was large enough that he would have to be careful not to extend past the tunnel anywhere.

Two of the local Lottl came into the badlands with them to return the mountbeasts to Von's portal. The beasts would eat the local grasses, but made it plain they didn't much like them. The animals were difficult all the way. Dracht said they always had been hard to handle in an unfamiliar place when that lack of familiarity was from a very different type of landscape and/or vegetation. They would know they were being returned to Kholworld by the Lottl so would not be so difficult.

Those two Lottl would wait a few minutes, then remove the director crystals to the portal, thus closing it permanently. Var studied it carefully and noted again that

Khekth was truly intelligent to have been able to figure how to make it from Nighkt back to Kholworld. Now he could construct portals anywhere for the Lottl, should they wish it. There were areas on Kholworld they would find very suitable and having the portals in Nighkt would allow them total control of the passings back and forth, the only real drawback being that they would have to be placed in areas such as this, areas the Lottl considered badlands.

Var and Dracht exchanged good fortunes with the Lottl and went through to a dank underroom cut into rock. They waited until their eyes adjusted to the darkness and the portal closed behind them.

"Khekth will know the portal has closed," Var whispered. "He can't know if it is because of us or if something happened in Nighkt that caused it to close.

"Note that there are crystals here that would open a small portal to Nighkt. He went from here to there with the short-term portal, carrying the crystals to open the portal from that end ... he took a very dangerous chance. Had he not been able to open the portal there he would have been trapped!"

"No, he already had the one in Gretlz. He might have left a locator beacon thing there so he could find it.

"If he knows this one is closed he'll have to come check it out. If we move his crystals here he'll know something's happening and that we're involved."

"I believe the portal there will have a director crystal in common here or he couldn't have them in both places. I noted that when I inspected the one in Nighkt. It will be in this sequence here." He closely studied the crystals a moment, then grinned. He worked a rock loose from the wall directly above the crystal and used it to smash it, embedding a small piece of it in the rock which he rolled to where it would stop had it actually dropped from the wall.

"That would close both portals. Khekth has the worst luck!

"I felt a seeker there. He will be coming to determine what went wrong to close the portal. We must hide somewhere."

"This is a carved room. There's no place to hide here. There's the one door that will be barred from the outside."

"I can remove the bar with a piece of the wire I carry," Var said. He moved to the tiny window in the door, ran his hands along the inside, then made a hook on a piece of the wire and dropped it through the window to catch the bar.

"Offer encouragement to the fates that there is no stoplock on the bar!" Var said and slowly pulled the wire. It raised the bar and they heard the iron rod drop.

Dracht quickly pushed the door open, they exited the room and Var replaced the rod before they went quickly along a short hall. Var put his hand up and motioned for Dracht to step into a side room. He followed and reclosed the door they had opened to enter. Var waved for Dracht to move behind the granite wall and he pressed close behind. Dracht knew that the small crystals that made up granite would interfere with a weak seeker spell so would serve to hide them.

Someone passed the door to their hideaway and they soon heard the rod being lifted out of the holder brackets on the door to the portal room. There was silence for a moment, then a pale light shone against the hallway wall with a shadow that moved across it several times.

When they heard Khekth swear they went quietly out and up the stairs into a bright empty room. They could hear people in the next room, so Var motioned to the open balcony door and they went out there.

It was a straight drop from that balcony to jagged rocks, perhaps eight meters below. Dracht shrugged and began looking for a way down. There was nothing.

Var motioned Dracht to the side as someone came into the room. Dracht began removing his clothing. Var nodded and did the same, then they tied the garments together and around the balustrade. Dracht made a loop tie and took the wire from Var to hook through the slip, then tied a cloth to the end of the wire. It was about three meters above the rocks.

Dracht motioned for Var to slip down the garment rope, then followed, grabbing the cloth near the bottom and dropping the last meter and a half, holding it, which untied the garments around the balustrade.

Dracht scooped up the garments and they moved into a dense bank of bushes against the side of the castle to put their clothes back on. Var held up a hand when Dracht started to move out of the bushes and they waited until Khekth came to look out from the balcony. There was no evidence anyone had come out there and the people in the room beyond would tell him no one had come through, so he would assume there was an unfortunate accident when a loosened stone dropped from the crude wall.

After about a quarter hour Var and Dracht made their way to the side of the castle and up onto the road a fifth of a kilometer toward the village. They went into the village and took a room at the inn, then made arrangements to go to the nearby fishermen's islands, purportedly to purchase fish.

They met Von the next day and made a few plans. Von had Var's power crystal and a few other things he'd requested.

"It's a good thing you gave me the secret code to give King Narjur or I'd be warming a seat in the dungeons for trying to get into your private quarters! He is not someone to trifle with!" Von reported.

"There are no dungeons, but you would have very definitely been detained until I returned. If I never returned there would have been some very strong suspicions leveled against you. It is certain you would never leave whatever place they were holding you! We must find a way to get to Khekth that does not involve placing the innocent people here in danger."

"Some of the people here aren't nearly that innocent," Dracht pointed out.

"Which is why I so clearly stated that we must protect the ones who are! We must protect the *innocent* people here. The others have chosen their fate."

Chapter eight

"Well, I have my own power crystal, so Khekth won't have an easy time of it," Var said. "He will try to get to Gretlz, now that the portal is closed. I suspect he will have done something to draw me here, he would use the portal to go to Nighkt, I would find he is *not* here and would return to Fendrz, *then* he would go to Gretlz and have the time to start another scheme. He now can't hide in Nighkt so will ... I wonder!"

"Yeah," Dracht sneered. "What if he's already done something to bring you here and now he can't hide!"

"He can't hide so long as he has that power crystal with him," Von corrected. "To hide, he will have to deactivate it, which means putting it inside an ivory and crystal box and submerging it in a vat of mercury!"

"And he will have no power again without that crystal unless he can find another," Var said. "Let's say he will not have much power without *a* power crystal.

"If he tries to leave with the crystal we can use it to follow him anywhere. If he has ... he would expect me to try to locate him, regardless. If I can locate that crystal he will try to take it with him. If not it is already deactivated."

He took out a special seeker crystal and sat to concentrate. After only a moment he said, "He has the crystal with him. He is on the sea! He has not gone far, but he is on the sea heading toward Gretlz. He knows I have used the spell to locate him and should be greatly worried about that because he has no protection on the sea of a type he has on land. There is no place to hide.

"He will be on a trader. That was done to try to move as a normal trader without attracting undue attention. Traders are relatively slow. We can use a fast communications boat to overtake them in a few hours. We must leave immediately."

They went to the nearby docks and used Var's standing with Fendrz, who owned the islands, to commandeer the courier boat, which was there to deliver messages to and from other countries. They were en route in less than half an hour.

"It'll be kinda close," Captain Merck warned. "We've got a good backwind, but so do they and they're gettin' fairly close to possible landin's at Darksea and Resintree Atoll."

"Aren't those among the dangerous ports?" Dracht asked. "I've heard there are obstructions that can sink a ship if a captain is at all careless."

"At some times of the year when they get cross winds or strong winds that there's true," Capt. Merck said. "This time of year there ain't any big problem. Visibility's right good and there's no wind problem."

Var grinned and set up his power crystal and three seeker crystals. He concentrated and a shadowy form of a ship with an island low on the horizon floated over the power crystal. The water was suddenly becoming fuzzy toward the island.

"Ah!" Von cried. "You are Lord of Fogs!"

"Uh-huh," Dracht agreed. "The visibility there is going to suddenly become very bad for this time of the year! A very heavy sea fog is going to cover the area!"

They were silent for awhile until the entire scene floating there was a white fog. Var then placed his power crystal back in its carrier. "The fog will stay the day and night. Captain, how long until we arrive in the area of that ship?"

"Two, two and a half hours," Capt. Merck replied.

"Shall we take a short nap so that we will be refreshed for the coming confrontation?" Var suggested.

"The fog's right dead ahead," Capt. Merck announced.

Var nodded. He said that Khekth had twice sent the locator seeker spell and knew they were there. He would try to hide in the fog.

"Hide in the fog? From *you?!*" Von cried.

"He doesn't know Var's talent is with the fog," Dracht answered. "He'll think the fog's merely another bit of the ill fortune he's cursed with lately.

"Well, it is, really, seeing Var's the ill fortune cursing him.

"What do we do now, Var?"

"It is perhaps an hour before the darkness. I'll remove the fog except very close to the ship, during the night, then can remove the last with the dawnlight. We will be well rested then, but I would wager a large sum that Khekth will certainly not be. He is using the crystal to try to produce enough light for navigation, but that will not work. The fog simply throws the light back at him."

"I can't sleep until the dawn, starting now!" Dracht complained. "Captain, do you play targets?"

"Targets? No," Capt. Merck replied. "Now, rolling the cubes, I've been known to show a fondness for and I do happen to have a deck of numbers-up cards!"

"Ah!" Dracht exclaimed. "And do you have a large amount to use on a game such as cutthroat or kings over queens?"

"I predict it'll be you who'll have need of cash!" Capt. Merck replied, happily.

The two sat at the navigation chart table and Capt. Merck produced the cards. They laughed and joked late into the night as they played while Von and Var studied a book Von had brought along.

The card game ended with Dracht owing Capt. Merck ten silvers, which showed that both were very skilled players.

Then they slept.

"Khekth has managed to move a bit, but no captain is going to allow his ship to be taken into those narrows under bad visibility conditions," Var reported. "Captain Merck, I will not ask you to remain here for this confrontation. We may, none of us, survive it."

"Wasn't plannin' to live forever nohow," Capt. Merck replied. "I been in some tight-n's. People say I'm charmed, so maybe I'll be good luck.

"What's ter do?"

"Move us close to that rocky jut to starboard and stay out of sight. Von, stay in the wheelhouse. Dracht, stay back and low.

"I'll remove the fog and they will be only a few meters past the jut. We are no more than fifty meters from them here and will be perhaps twenty five meters when I remove the fog.

"Captain, have the boat pointed to that second high point of the rocks. I will be in the center of the foredeck.

"Von, you can contain the focus of the seeker and I will have a seeker linked with yours, which will give me some advantage with my power crystal.

"Dracht, all I can ask is that you watch for an opportunity to distract Khekth. If he loses his concentration for only one second I can contain his power and we will win.

"This is not a certain outcome we can look forward to. He's powerful and I do not have the confidence I project. I can protect us if he's not allowed to focus on an individual and that would have to be me. The rest must distract him."

Dracht grunted, Capt. Merck nodded and Von looked grim. Var said to get the play on the stage and moved to the center of the foredeck to place his power crystal and concentrate. As their boat reached its spot before the rock jut the fog began to thin to show the trader ship a mere twenty meters away with Khekth standing among several sailors. He was standing on something that left only his head above the others.

"You've crossed my path for the last time, Herkth!" he screeched wildly. "I will *end* your interference!"

"Your stupid schemes are what will be ended here," Var returned, calmly. "You are insane. You have caused more than enough grief to too many innocent people. Your use of those sailors who have no part in this proves beyond doubt what you are."

"You do not fool me! You would have the power instead of me, but that *will not* happen!"

"I wish no power, because power is never held for long without responsibility. I have enough responsibility in my life now."

"You lie! Anyone wants power! Only the stronger may hold it! I am the stronger! You will loose!"

He raised the light thrower and fired it at Var, whose power crystal drew it. Var heard Dracht swear behind him, but dared not look. Dracht said he was going to use a light thrower against Khekth, but that wouldn't be any good.

Khekth concentrated on his crystal so Dracht fired the light thrower at him and he looked his fury back at him, but didn't lose his concentration on Var.

"Get him talking!" Dracht hissed.

Var asked if Khekth had discovered the secret of Nighkt and Khekth replied that Nighkt didn't have any secrets to him, at which Var laughed. Von moved into view for a second at Dracht's urging and Khekth noticed him.

That split his concentration for a second, but not enough.

"Oh, Nighkt has an enormous secret that you don't have the power to discover, but which even a young apprentice found," Var called. "Perhaps you should consider exactly how much power you do possess!"

"There is no secret there!" Khekth screamed. He rose a little bit higher above the sailors, then suddenly pitched backward, an iron crossbow bolt through his head.

"I was getting bored with the silly speeches," Dracht said. "Sometimes the older ways are the best."

"Most effective, anyway," Von agreed, coming out onto the deck. "This ends the problem and bypasses the actual fact you would have so much internal discussion before you took final action against such as Khekth.

"I would, too. I would have to build up the courage to act."

"Var is too civilized and he cares too much about morality," Dracht said. "He couldn't do anything to kill or even hurt that mountbeast plop. He would wait until Khekth had done something to attack the innocent people around him, then would kill him, then agonize for decades because he had hesitated and allowed an innocent person to be hurt.

"I'm not so civilized. I'm direct. He was a danger to everyone around him, so I ended the danger. I won't agonize over killing some animal with the mad-shakes before he could kill a lot of other people. He's gone and we're better for it.

"Var, I suggest you go over there and collect the crystals and such before someone gets hurt fooling with them. I'll handle the honors of tying a rock to Khekth and dumping him overboard in deep water where he can make the clawpinchers and fishes that feed on his carcass sick.

"I want to get home, report to King Narj and go to Nighkt – or rather, Lottlland – to find a nice little place where I can go to lay around and get fat and lazy."

"Hah!" Var retorted. "You want to go home, find a new *lady* and go to Lottlland to lay around and ... lay around."

"There is that! Let's say it will not greatly disturb me if she doesn't quite fit the finer definition of 'lady'."

They laughed and joked while they did exactly what Dracht had suggested, then headed for Fendrz.

Var looked out over the balcony and sighed. Narj and Yu had just "locked the chains" in a very festive ceremony and Fendrz and Treglz were now East and West Freglz, with Freeland between. It was the first single kingdom on Kholworld that had no direct connection.

Var had hoped Vardan Fekth would be named Vardan of the Realm, but he was.

Dracht, true to his goal, had found a very attractive "working lady" to accompany him to Lottlland for a tenthcycle of relaxation in a small pleasant cabin in the badlands near the stream. Var had visited and found that Von had supplied Dracht with a communications crystal and taught him how to use it. There were several of the Lottl units in and out of the place and Dracht said the hardest thing to accept was that privacy was non-existent, but that he and Djeana, his "friend", were now used to the Lottl even climbing into the bed with them to ask what they were doing – and why. They were merely curious and it really had no meaning to them, past the biological facts. They would answer any question with total candor and expected no less of others.

"You get used to it," Dracht related. "I'm no longer uncomfortable explaining things I would never even mention to another Khol.

"Well, I suppose you can now lay around and be bored with your lot in life now. You've lived the adventure part!"

It was neither the first nor the last time Dracht was wrong.

C. D. Moultons works are available on most major outlets as printed or e-books. CD writes the CD Grimes, PI mysteries, the Det. Lt. Nick Storie mysteries, the Clint Faraday mysteries, the Flight of the Maita science fiction series, books on orchid culture and many others of many types. Mystery, adventure, intrigue, science fiction, fantasy, paranormal, mild erotica, and factual.